After catching   :h
another alpha,   et
space away before ne does some....g   'll
regret—like let the man remain in his life. He
heads up to the little used family lake house,
hoping it's enough distance between him and a
cheating ex.

Too bad his younger omega brother has handed
a key to that lake house to a friend who needs to
cycle off his heat-blocking drugs. Bellamy Carter
has waited too long and his body is struggling.
He's on the cusp of a wild heat—brought on by
suppressing his nature too long. By the time he
walks into the lake house, he's in full heat... and
there's a sexy alpha across the room who's more
than willing to assist.

Quinn is enslaved by the instinct and goes into
full rut. The pair spend several days in bed,
sating the animal need within them both. When
it's over, they part awkwardly, still little more
than strangers. Unsure how they feel about each
other and the bond they've already seemed to
forge, it's not until they see each other again that
they realize it wasn't just a wild heat, but
something more.

But will life get into the way of their happily ever
after?

One Wild Heat

Alphas of the Western Provinces

One Wild Heat

AN OMEGAVERSE BOOK

Kelex

A TWISTED E PUBLISHING BOOK

One Wild Heat
Alphas of the Western Provinces, 1
Copyright © 2019 by Kelex

Cover design by K Designs
All cover art and logo copyright © 2019, Twisted E-Publishing, LLC

ISBN: 9781099463464

Dedication

Prior to writing this book, I'd lapsed into a dark depression that didn't feel surmountable. I wasn't able to read, write... I wasn't able to do much of anything.

Finally, I forced myself to type some words onto the page.

I couldn't face the mountain of a story that was on my agenda. It was just too big.

And this is the story that came.
It helped pull me out of the abyss and back to the world of the living.

So, this dedication is to all those out there struggling with depression and other mental illnesses.

You're not alone.

The world might feel like a dark place sometimes, and the mountains too immense to climb, but maybe there's another path through.

One Wild Heat

Kelex

Author's Note:

While this *is* an Omegaverse book, it's the first book
in a new series
based in the <u>same world</u> as
His Surrogate Omega (Omega Quadrant, 1).

Wilder and Avery's story *is* coming.
It was the mountain I wasn't ready to climb.

I'm ready now.

*

Side note… if you're a little curious about the heat
blocking drugs omegas use during their heats, I wrote
a little blog post explaining the differences...

http://www.authorkelex.com/2019/05/omegaverse-
faq-what-are-these-heat.html

One Wild Heat

Kelex

After the Great Catastrophe, civilization as many knew ceased to exist. Cities burned. Continents reshaped. Billions were wiped away from the face of the planet. Only a handful were left behind to restart anew.

But those who began again were changed. The savagery that had ended life also left an imprint on those who remained, changing them in ways they didn't quite understand.

Life, as it always does, goes on. The new world was built on the skeleton of nations forgotten.

Thousands of years later, it now looks and feels much like it did before the world trembled and was nearly lost.

Only, it's not the same at all...

One Wild Heat

Chapter One

Downtown Fort Seattle
Western Provinces
McCreary Towers

"We've finally gotten the go-ahead to purchase Barrington Industries," Quinn McCreary stated as he strode into his grandfather's glass-walled office. Fort Seattle was dark and stormy in the background, the setting sun barely visible through the clouds. He eyed his younger brother, Beau, and his grandfather, Tolliver, before heading for the bar cart. He poured himself a stiff drink and drained half the glass before turning back to them. "I know what we said in the meetings, but I *do* think it would be beneficial to break them up into smaller pieces before we begin selling everything off."

"Agreed," Tolliver was quick to reply. Too quick. Apparently, his grandfather had had no intention of following through with his promise.

"We told their board we wouldn't do that," Beau said, lifting a brow as he eyed Quinn.

"Sometimes we must say what they need to hear in order to get them to sign their name to the dotted line…" Tolliver sized Beau up a moment before shaking his head and glancing at Quinn. "At least *one* of my grandsons understands that."

Beau rolled his eyes and gazed at Quinn. "And the hundreds of people who'll likely lose their jobs?"

"Just a part of doing business," Quinn murmured.

"When did you become so cold-hearted, brother?" Without waiting for an answer, Beau turned to their grandfather. "Weren't you just talking to me of the family legacy? Just what *is* that? Clearly not honor."

Tolliver McCreary scoffed, lifting one thick brow. "I did not build this company by playing fair. I've done far worse along the way."

"So, because you've done worse, this doesn't rate in comparison?" Beau blasted. "We should just ignore the feeling in our guts and move on?"

"Beau!" Quinn snapped, quieting his brother. "Yes, there *will* be some job losses at the onset, but by breaking up the conglomerate into smaller pieces, it'll be easier for us to sell them and generate a larger profit. You know full well they're mismanaging the smaller operations… because they'd grown *too large*. They can no longer see the big picture. In the long term, there will likely be *more* jobs added—once we sell them to those who *can* manage them properly. This is a *good* thing."

"I thought we'd discussed reviewing the individual businesses and working to improve upon their performance," Beau snapped. "Give the company a chance."

"Of course we discussed it, but we never agreed that was what we *would* do," Quinn told his brother. "We discussed many possibilities… and after careful analysis, I think this is our best option. The investment of time and manpower won't equal any more profit than we would get selling it off. Piece by piece."

"And what happens when someone comes for *our* company? Breaks it into smaller pieces and sells it off to the highest bidder?" Beau asked.

"As long as I have Quinn to help me lead the way, I won't have that problem," Tolliver said, smiling. He leaned forward in his chair and rested his elbows on his desk. "Now, on to a new topic. Have you heard about Abel Macklin's health issues?"

"Of course I've heard," Quinn murmured, curious why his grandfather was bringing the topic up.

"I know I wasn't understanding of your relationship with Abel's son at first… but upon reflection, I think a marriage to your beta might benefit *both* families, Quinn."

Quinn McCreary lifted his stare to his grandfather, shock washing through him.

It took a few seconds for his mind to reboot and begin to digest what his grandfather was suggesting. Yes, Charles was the heir to a massive fortune, which included their competitor, Ross-Macklin Investments… but he had been a smokescreen to avoid conversations such as this. They'd both decided to share a bed and their lives for a while—warding off questions of marriage, because who in their right minds would expect them to mate?

"He's a beta," Quinn murmured, wondering if senility was finally creeping into his grandfather's whip-smart mind. "He can't carry my children."

"There's no law against it. Marriage between an alpha and a beta," Tolliver McCreary said as he sat back in his high-backed office chair, the swirl of dark storm clouds behind him. "You can mate whoever you choose. Isn't that what all those idiotic marches were all about decades before? Freedom to love who you want? Rights and privileges?"

"That wasn't exactly it, Grandfather," Beau interjected. "It was omega rights, and you know full well that's what it was."

"If these omegas want to be treated as equal and be given choices in who they bond with, then I say we alphas should have the freedom to choose, too," Tolliver announced before eyeing Quinn. "These things go both ways."

Quinn stiffened, searching his mind for a reasonable reason to end the conversation. Simply saying he didn't love Charles wouldn't be good enough for his grandfather. Love was a luxury in Tolliver's mind, one men like them couldn't afford.

Tolliver continued his train of thought. "Charles will need someone strong of mind and will to help him navigate the business once he becomes head of that family. From what I've seen—he can't do it on his own. He'd squander it all if given the liberty to do so."

"His father isn't even dead yet," Quinn snapped. "And you're here discussing picking his carcass."

"Don't be so crass," his grandfather spat.

"And you're not being crass?"

"I'm being pragmatic. No. He's not dead yet, but it's only a matter of time. Likely, it'll be a slow decline... to the point Charles might gain more and more control before his father passes," Tolliver said. "He'll need someone he trusts to guide him, Quinn. That should be you."

"And what of my bond-mate? What of children? Charles cannot give me those—and considering how hard you've pressed me to mate and give you great-grandchildren, I'm surprised you're making this suggestion," Quinn stated.

"Hell, he recently suggested I go take a tour of the Eastern Provinces and attend some of their Omega Balls, in search of a mate myself," Beau said to Quinn.

"Is it so wrong that I want to go to my grave knowing you boys have begun the next generation of McCrearys? We can trace our lineage from *before* the Great Catastrophe, before the near destruction of this world. It was *our* ancestors who rebuilt civilization as we know it now. We were survivors then, and we are survivors now. I won't die wondering if my line will end with you lot."

"Which only makes it odder that you suggest I mate *a beta*," Quinn stated. "How am I supposed to begin a new generation with a male who could bear me no children?"

Tolliver scoffed, waving a hand before him. "As if you couldn't use a surrogate to breed with." He paused, an odd look crossing his face. "Or better yet, build yourself a harem like they had years before."

"A harem?" Quinn eyed Beau before turning to his grandfather and wondering if the old man really was losing it. "I will *not* dishonor my bond-mate by mating with a beta and suggesting he become a member of my harem. The idea is ludicrous."

"You speak as if you've already met this omega. You haven't. Thanks to the omega rights laws, even if you did, they could hide from you, or better yet, refuse the mating." Quinn's grandfather sat back deeper into his chair and bridged his hands together over his barrel chest. "My great-grandfather, Orem, had a harem… and a *bevy* of children. He mated a beta *and* multiple omegas—and thanks to him, we have many lines of McCrearys throughout these Western

Provinces." Tolliver looked outside, at the rain streaking down the glass outer walls of his office. "Maybe I should've had a harem myself. Maybe then I would be surrounded by generations of children instead of worrying about our future."

"Harems are outlawed," Beau reminded their grandfather.

"Not when I was young, no," Tolliver murmured. "Of course, many people eyed them with distain as I was growing up. They were falling out of favor—the Eastern Provinces outlawed them a century or more before we did. Imagine… *they* were ahead of the curve on that one." Their grandfather smiled to himself. "I had the chance to marry more than one omega… and I nearly did. It's one of my deepest regrets that I didn't."

Beau glanced at Quinn, a worried look on his face. Quinn had never heard his grandfather speak like this… ruminating and filled with emotion. The man was tough as nails and rarely showed much of a softer side.

Tolliver smiled, turning to face his grandsons. "I bet I sound like a crazy, old fool, don't I?

"Perhaps just a little," Quinn murmured.

Tolliver leaned his elbows on his desk and eyed Quinn. "Think it over. You and Charles are well suited. He'll need a strong alpha to guide him… his family is beyond wealthy, my boy. It would be a good union."

"What about love, Grandfather?" Beau asked.

Quinn rolled his eyes. There it was. *Love.* His younger brother, the fool.

"Love is a commodity we are too poor to afford. No matter how wealthy we are." Their grandfather paused, a wistful look on his face. "My father told me that and in my youth, I thought him terrible. But he was right. Love fades. Or it dies." He paused again, looking haunted. Quinn had never met his grandpapa. Tolliver's omega had died years before he was born, and the old man rarely spoke on the subject. Was that man the reason for that look? "In time, you'll see that power is the only thing that matters," Tolliver answered, his face twisting angrily. "Money buys power. Influence. Satiates lust. Everything an alpha needs in this world."

Quinn heard the pain lingering in Tolliver's words and knew there was more to that story. He also knew he'd likely never hear it. Rising from his seat across from his grandfather's desk, he smiled wanly at the old man. "I'll consider it. Charles, that is," he lied, knowing full well he wasn't mating his beta.

"Good," the old man replied, looking satisfied.

"I've got some work to get caught up on before the weekend." He bowed to their patriarch before heading for the door. "Be well, Grandfather."

"I should go, too," Beau said, saluting the old man.

"Be safe, my boys," Tolliver said as they exited.

Quinn nodded to Tolliver's assistant as he slowly sauntered toward the elevator, awaiting his brother to move closer. As soon as they were out of earshot, Beau turned to him. "This isn't the first time he's spouted nonsense. I think he's losing it."

"My gods, Beau, he's nearly ninety. Considering that, his mental state is *outstanding*." Quinn sighed inwardly, knowing that there was something shifting in their grandfather but he refused to speak it aloud. *A little slip. That's all it had been.*

"As of late, I've been spending a lot of time with him. It's gotten far worse than talk of mating betas and harems." Beau glanced back at the closed office doors, his eyes narrowing some before he turned back to Quinn. "He's not himself."

"He was simply reminiscing a bygone era."

"*This* time."

"I would imagine standing at the end of a long life gives anyone pause." Quinn glanced around, making sure no one was overhearing his younger brother call their grandfather's logic into question. "I'm sure I'll look back once I'm where he is and think of the past. Wonder if I've lived a good life."

Beau glared. "And do you think you'll be happy with what you see when you do?"

Quinn narrowed his eyes, knowing full well it was a dig about Barrington Industries. "Business is business, brother."

"I'd much rather think I lived an honorable life, one where I delivered on promises made."

"Always the crusader." Quinn saw the hardy idealism on his brother's face and knew he'd once worn it, as well. Several years after beginning work for his grandfather it had slowly washed away, leaving a jaded businessman in the place of the boy. A little piece of him didn't want Beau to lose that same quality. He also didn't want to be the one to rob his brother of it. "I'll review the data and see if we can't find a middle road."

Beau's smile was nearly infectious. Quinn had to work hard not to return the show of emotion. He let his mind wander back to the suggestion old Tolliver had just made. That made him wince in pain once more.

Mate Charles? *Hardly*.

The elevator quietly pinged before the double doors opened to an empty car. They both stepped inside. His brother began to speak again as the doors closed and they began their descent.

"About this thing with Charles…"

Quinn lifted a hand. "Trust me… I don't agree with Grandfather there. I won't be mating him."

"Good," Beau said, his face darkening. "But there's more to it. There's something I've been meaning to tell you… and I didn't know how."

Quinn stiffened, already sensing what his brother might say. Whispers had already gotten to him. "Tell me."

****

The following morning…

"The key, as promised. I *finally* found it. Go me!"

Bellamy Carter lifted his stare, seeing his freedom dangling from the keychain in Tanner's hand. Light played off the puddles outside the plate glass window of the café and glinted on the stainless steel of the key. He reached up and grasped it, sighing slightly as soon as it was in his hand. "Thanks… I was starting to worry you wouldn't find it in time."

"Key? For what?" Bellamy's friend and sometimes lover, Fitz, asked as he lifted one of his thick brows.

Bellamy had tried to find a way to bring up the subject all through breakfast and had failed.

Luckily Tanner answered for him. "B needs some time away, so I'm letting him use my family's lake house for a long weekend because I'm an awesome friend and have the connections." Tanner slid into the booth across from Bellamy, leaning against Fitz. He reached onto Fitz's plate and snagged a piece of the alpha's bacon and popped it into his mouth.

Fitz glared at Tanner for a moment before turning his worried gaze toward Bellamy. "Time away? When?"

"Soon," Bellamy answered before turning his attention back to his breakfast.

Fitz put his fork down and stared. "*This* weekend?"

Bellamy met the alpha's disappointed stare. He wasn't ready for this conversation, especially with Tanner paying such close attention. He looked between the pair before nodding. "Yes."

"Alone?" the alpha prodded.

"Fitz… I *am* capable of being alone on occasion," Bellamy murmured. "I don't always need a big, bad alpha around to protect me."

An uncomfortable silence fell over the table— emanating from the alpha at the table. Bellamy turned to glare at Tanner, who shrugged and slid back out of the booth, gratefully getting the hint. "While I would like nothing better than to remain here and listen to this stimulating conversation, I think it's time for me to be off to the races. People to see, things to paint. Fitz, if you need something to do this weekend, you could head on down to the Row—I'm sure you could find some sad, needy omega to fuck there." Tanner brushed a hand through Fitz's hair. "In those circles, *someone* just might find you attractive."

Fitz glared. "Didn't I hear you were down there last heat cycle? I'm not interested in fucking you, McCreary."

Tanner grinned widely as he pulled his hand back. "Oh, if you were *ever* that lucky… you'd *never* survive a heat with me. Meds or no meds."

Fitz scoffed and rolled his eyes. Tanner paused before reaching into his pocket and pulling out a folded piece of paper. Tanner slid it across the table toward Bellamy. "Security codes—plus a map. Once you get into the mountains, cell phones don't like to work so well. If you're using GPS, it could crap out on you on the way."

"Thanks," Bellamy said, grabbing the folded sheet and tucking it into one pocket. For once, his very irresponsible friend was being quite responsible. Given the weight of the situation, he appreciated it.

"By the way… I tossed a bag into the car. I picked you up one of my favorite toys. A vibrating egg that's attached to a sleeve by a cord. They both pulse in time with one another and will send you to the stratosphere—*trust me.*"

"TMI," Fitz murmured.

Tanner gave Fitz another glare before turning, flipping his long, unruly hair over one shoulder, and leaving. Fitz's face grew red as he watched Tanner's ass swish away.

And even redder when he realized Bellamy had caught him.

As soon as their friend was out of earshot, Fitz turned that angry glare back his way. "Were you planning to invite me?"

"No," Bellamy murmured, looking down at his plate. He pushed it back, no longer hungry.

"I thought we would be spending this weekend together. Like the last few."

Bellamy faced Fitz's anger. He should've told the alpha sooner, but he hadn't had the heart. "I appreciate all the help you've been giving me." He'd been on the heat blocker too long, and it was beginning to fail him. Unable to find a safe space to cycle off, he'd endured the growing lust. Fitz had been in the right place, at the right time one month... and it had been hot, sexy, and wonderful, and had eased the ache within better than the toys he'd been using. One month had turned into several... and he'd gotten lazy about doing what he needed to do.

"Is this because of what I said last time?"

I love you.

The words had come from Fitz's lips as he'd come, and it had terrified Bellamy. Fitz had been a bandage for a bad situation. It was time for Bellamy to purge his system and put them both on equal footing again.

They were friends. Friends with benefits, sure, but they could never be more than that.

"It's been about four years since I've had a break from the meds. I'm supposed to have one every year or two. I *need* this." He'd relied on the heat blocker for far too long. If he pushed it much farther, it could stop working completely and he *definitely* didn't need that.

"I could've helped you," Fitz murmured as he leaned over the table a little more. "If you'd bothered telling me."

Bellamy ignored the tone to Fitz's voice. "Have you ever been in a room with an omega in full heat?"

Fitz leaned back in the booth and eyed him. "No… but I've helped you through *plenty* of heats over these months."

"And I'm appreciative of that. But those weren't full heats. Nowhere close. If you went into full rut, things could get forgotten in the frenzy." *Like condoms.* "I'm not chancing it." Bellamy laid the key on the table. "Tan's family's lake house is out in the middle of nowhere. It's gated and has alarms. He says they never go up there, so it sits empty most of the year."

"Leave it to the McCrearys to have nice things they never use."

Bellamy ignored Fitz's comment. "Regardless, I'll be safe there, and I can endure it for one weekend. Alone."

Fitz frowned. "I don't like the idea of you being up there by yourself. *Suffering.*"

Bellamy reached across the table and rested his hand on Fitz's. "You're a good friend. And I appreciate all the help you've given me these past months." He smiled wanly. Fitz wasn't *his* alpha, but there were plenty of times he'd wished the man was. Fitz was everything he'd want in a mate. Kind. Considerate. Protective. Supportive. "But I need to do this alone. It's one heat. One long weekend. I can manage by myself."

Fitz eyed him a moment before sighing. The alpha shook his head and turned away. Bellamy knew Fitz truly had feelings for him, but in their world, it was all about the bonded pair. He cared for the alpha, but not in the same way. He and Fitz weren't bond-mates and could never be together.

Not for forever, anyway. They'd both walked in knowing that, but somewhere along the way Fitz had gotten lost—which was the main reason Bellamy needed to be alone that weekend. If Fitz experienced a full heat and rut, the alpha might grow too attached.

He already is.

Bellamy watched the emotions crossing Fitz's face before he lifted his fork again and returned to eating. Bellamy did the same, very ready to get on the way.

"How are you getting up there?"

"Tanner let me borrow his car," Bellamy answered. "I had a mechanic check it over yesterday. Oil's been changed, and it's all gassed up."

Fitz's face screwed up, just like it did whenever the omega was mentioned. The fact that the rich omega was helping Bellamy escape town was likely not helping Fitz's dislike of Tanner McCreary. "When are you leaving?"

Bellamy smiled. "Right after breakfast."

Fitz's brows shot up. "So soon?"

"I want to get up there well before my heat hits," Bellamy answered. "It's likely going to come early… between being so long and being off meds."

"How far is this place?"

"Should take me about three and a half hours according to Tanner," Bellamy answered, seeing the worry crossing Fitz's face. "I plan to stop at a small supermarket in a little town Tanner told me about and pick up some necessities, not that I'll likely eat much."

"You can't go four days without eating or drinking," Fitz spat.

"I won't. I'm going to pick up bottled water and meal bars at the store—and keep them by the bed. Easy enough."

"There'll be no one there to tend to you after," Fitz argued. After a full heat-rut, instinct roared inside the alpha to soothe and comfort the omega. Even milder heats, like those he had on meds, caused an alpha's instinct to kick in. It was a chemical reaction… a way the alpha proved he would provide and care for the omega once full with child. It was all an odd dance, one Bellamy wasn't rushing to see any time soon.

He had a career to focus on.

The alpha lifted his stare again, meeting Bellamy's. "Text me when you get there so I know you're okay. Again when you leave to come home." He paused. "And if you need *anything*. No matter the time… I'll be there as soon as I can if you need me."

Bellamy smiled slightly. "I know you would."

They finished up their meals, and Bellamy grabbed the check before Fitz could reach it. "My treat."

Fitz eyed him, concern in his aquamarine eyes. "Are you sure you don't want me to come with you?"

"I'm *quite* sure," Bellamy murmured.

After he paid, he let Fitz walk him to Tanner's borrowed car. Before Bellamy could say his goodbyes, the alpha drew him close and pressed a kiss to his lips.

"I'll miss you," Fitz whispered as he drew away.

"Fitz… you know we can't be mor—"

The alpha pressed a finger against his lips, quieting him. "There's no law that says I can't love you. Bonded or not, I love you, Bellamy."

"I love you, too, Fitz. Just not in the same way you love me," he whispered back, hating that he was hurting a man who cared so deeply. Fitz was his best friend. Confidante. Lover. The alpha was his rock, but there was no passion there. No deep abiding love. Bellamy wanted the kind of fire only a bonded pair could have. Fitz deserved that, too. "Somewhere out in the world, there's an omega who will love you the way you deserve to be loved. Because you *so* deserve to be loved, Fitz. With someone's whole heart."

Fitz eyed him, smiling wanly. They'd had this conversation before, maybe not quite as blunt and plainly. "Just not *your* heart."

Bellamy frowned, despising the broken tone to Fitz's voice. "You deserve better than me, Fitz."

"There is no better than you," Fitz said before stealing one more kiss.

"Don't you need to get to work," Bellamy murmured, again wishing things could be different for them. He hated feeling as if he was leading the alpha on, but he wasn't. He'd been honest from day one…

Maybe it's time to push him away. For his own good.

Fitz shook his head. "Yeah. Drive safe, okay?"

When he was done, he turned and stalked off, leaving Bellamy there to watch the man depart.

Why can't he be mine?

Bellamy shook his head and slid in behind the wheel. After turning on the engine, he stared out the window, a smile coming to his lips. He couldn't remember the last time he set out on an adventure alone. Even with the hell to come, he was excited.

Of course, while he was writhing in bed, in agony, he might change his mind about that.

Chapter Two

Victoria Highlands, North of Fort Seattle
A few hours later…

Quinn McCreary pulled his car up outside the front gates of the home he'd just left not an hour before. He tapped his hands on the steering wheel, wondering if he really wanted to face the confrontation to come yet knowing he might as well get it done and over with. After exiting the car, he clicked the fob on the keys in his pocket and slipped through the gates.

He kept to the shadows of the front garden, shushing the gardener as he passed the man. Yarrow lifted his brows, confused, but said nothing. He kept on tending to the flower beds, whistling. Quinn kept moving until he'd reached the house. Quietly, he opened the front door and stepped inside.

As soon as he made it to the second floor landing, he heard the sounds of sex coming from his bedroom. Quinn shoved the double doors open, just in time to see distant-cousin, Hagar, shoving his cock into Charles' ass. Hagar didn't stop moving as he gazed up at Quinn. He kept pumping into Charles as he smiled.

"Want to join us?"

Charles' head whipped to the side. His eyes rounded in terror as he saw Quinn. Scooting off Hagar's cock, he quickly crawled over the bed and raced closer. "It's not what you think…"

"It's not? So, you're *not* fucking my cousin?" Quinn asked calmly.

"Well, yes… but," Charles looked at Hagar and back up at Quinn. "I made a mistake. I knew it when I did it, but I didn't know how to stop myself. Can you forgive me?"

Quinn glared down at Charles, wanting to feel rage, but he couldn't summon it. "Look, we both knew this wasn't a forever kind of thing, but the least you could've done was not fuck my own flesh and blood… in *my* bed… right under my nose."

"I still say you climb in and make it a fun ménage," Hagar murmured, winking at Quinn. "I've heard that cock of yours is pretty impressive."

Quinn eyed Hagar and scowled. The leech had sucked enough blood out of their family. "Get out of my house."

Hagar sighed before shoving his cock back into the open vee of his pants. "Party pooper."

Quinn turned his attention back to Charles as soon as his cousin exited the bedroom. "Hagar? Really?"

"Quinn, darling, come on…" Charles cupped Quinn's cock through his pants and began to massage the shaft. "You're always working. I needed entertainment."

"*Entertainment?*"

"It's not like I planned it… it just… *happened*."

"Guess what else is *just happening?* You and I are done."

Charles chuckled. "Really now? Come on, lover. You're going to toss me out right now?" His smile faded, and he feigned a look of pain. "You know my father is unwell. My mind's filled with worry… I sought a little comfort… just from the wrong McCreary. We've all been there."

Quinn narrowed his eyes. For Charles to be so unemotional… but then, that was the main reason they'd gotten together in the first place. No strings. No entanglements. No emotions. Yet here was Charles, not letting go. *It's not like he actually loves me.* "As I said, it's over."

Charles turned and somehow forced tears to shimmer in his eyes.

"Take your crocodile tears elsewhere," Quinn murmured. "Maybe they'll work on someone else."

Charles glowered at him. "You'd really do this now? When I'm at my lowest? I needed you, and you weren't here. You're *never* here!"

Quinn ignored most of Charles' arguments, shaking his head. "You have one weekend to clear your shit out of here. When I get back home, I don't want to see you ever again. Do you understand me?"

He grabbed one of the go-bags he kept packed in case he needed to make a last-minute trip and added a couple of items before he turned to leave.

Charles pulled on his arm, stopping him in his tracks. "Come on, Quinn. Like you said, we both knew this wasn't forever. I can't be your bonded mate… so why does it matter? I wouldn't be upset to hear if you were screwing someone else."

Honestly, Quinn had been looking for a good opportunity to get Charles out of his bed even before his grandfather brought up that crazy idea of mating the man. Hagar had likely done him a favor. He looked down at the handsome beta and shook his head. "Had you come to me with a proposal… been honest from the start… and not fucked half the men in this town, thinking I wouldn't hear about it … but you hide… scurrying around in the dark… keeping secrets… because you *knew* it was wrong… and you think I won't be angry when I finally find proof of an affair?"

In my own fucking bed.

He'd have to burn the mattress. And the sheets. The gods only knew where Hagar's cock had been.

Quinn pulled his arm from Charles' grip. "I'll be back in a few days. You better clear out while I'm gone… because if you're still here when I get back… there *will* be hell to pay."

Charles frowned at him, a slight pout to the beta's lips. "Quinn… you know how good we are together. You can't do this. Let me make it right…" He walked closer. "I love you, Quinn."

No, you don't. Quinn wasn't falling for the beta's lies any longer. *Why am I even arguing with him? I don't need this bullshit in my life. Just walk away.* He turned and stalked toward the front door, ignoring Charles' cries for him to turn back.

Before he got to the front door, he heard his name called again, by someone else.

"Quinn?"

He paused at the sound of Hagar's voice. Turning, he glared at his cousin.

"Mind if I stay for a while? Your grandfather kicked me out of the villa."

Quinn's mouth dropped open at the utter gall of the man. He stared a moment, dumfounded, before he recaptured his wits. He stalked closer and pressed a finger to Hagar's chest. "Get the fuck out of my house."

Hagar shrugged, not looking too upset. He stuck his hands into his pockets and leisurely walked out.

"Quinn!" Charles screamed from the stairs.

He turned to look at the beta—who stood there naked, his semi-hard cock swaying between his legs.

"This *isn't* over. Not by a long shot."

Ignoring Charles, he headed for the door. As he exited the house, Quinn saw both his brother Beau and the back end of Hagar's car as it raced out of his circular drive. Quinn stopped beside the back of Beau's car and eyed his brother.

"From the speed of Hagar's escape, I would assume the deed is done?"

"It is," Quinn murmured, hating the hint of a smile on Beau's lips. They had *'I told you so'* written all over them. His brother hated Charles and for months had told him to kick the beta to the curb. "Thanks for volunteering to supervise the move out. I don't want to be here and have him try and lure me back—yet I don't want my house burned to the fucking ground, either."

Charles had some kind of supernatural power and had kept Quinn stuck in his web for far too long as it was. He needed distance.

"Where are you going for the weekend?"

"I think I might head up to the lake house. No one ever goes up there anymore. Mind telling grandfather I'll be away a few days?"

"No problem," Beau said. "This early in the year, it'll be cool up there. Too cold for the water. Maybe you should go somewhere tropical."

"I don't need to go in the water. I just need some peace and quiet. It's out in the middle of nowhere… so it should be perfect."

As if on cue, Charles came rushing out of the house, dressed in a tiny pair of briefs that showed off his trim, cut body. Tears shimmered in his eyes. "Quinn… we need to talk about this…"

Before Charles could get much closer, Beau slipped in between them. He glared down at the beta before looking over his shoulder. "Escape while you can, brother."

Quinn headed for his car and soon slid in behind the wheel as he heard Beau and Charles arguing behind him. Shaking his head, he started the engine and roared out of the drive. As he sped out of the gated community, he grabbed his ringing cell phone and saw his youngest brother Tanner's name on the screen. Shaking his head—and knowing he was in no mindset to hear from his rambling omega brother— he turned his phone off and tossed it into the backseat. No way was he going to let anyone make his shitty day any worse. Spending an hour listening to Tanner drone on about his weird friends before asking for money wasn't on the agenda.

He headed for the mountains.

To find some peace and quiet.

****

Later that afternoon…

After getting himself lost in the valley and driving in the wrong direction for a better part of an hour, Bellamy finally pulled into the lot for the small supermarket. He opened the driver's door and stood, stretching his arms above his head. A gust of wind whipped the door open wider and caused it to slightly ding a fancy red sports car parked beside him.

Hissing in fear, he pulled the door away and saw there appeared to be no damage. Then he looked around to see if anyone had spied his blunder and was relieved to see no one lurking around. Relieved, he relaxed some. Another gust whipped past him, strong enough to make him lean to one side. Pollen and new leaves floated from the neighboring trees, dancing through the air on the breeze. Glancing up, he saw the sky growing heavy and dark above.

Better hurry up and get outta here ASAP.

Bellamy closed the door and headed inside the market. It was much smaller than the ones he was used to in the city, but there was definitely a charm to it. He grabbed a basket and filled it with a little fresh fruit, even though he doubted he'd eat much of it. *There's always tonight.* His heat shouldn't start for another day, and then there was the day after his heat. He'd be starving by that point.

Bellamy felt a bit of his slick ease from his ass, and he froze. *Oh no.* It was a day and a half early. It had been too long since he'd been off-meds… and now it seemed he might start sooner than he'd anticipated. The storm was good enough reason to hurry. Slick was enough reason to bolt.

He quickly picked up a box of meal bars, as well as some broth and crackers to have for dinner that night, if he ate at all. Before he went to the cashier, he stopped for a case of bottled water. Just as he reached for it, a man moved in close, reaching for the same case.

"Sorry," Bellamy murmured, letting go. He rose to his full height and eyed the handsome man. The *familiar-looking,* handsome man.

The familiar-looking, handsome *alpha.*

A little more of Bellamy's slick eased from him, and he drew in a deep breath. The alpha inhaled deeply, his eyes widening some. He looked down at Bellamy, his body growing tense. "Take it," the alpha growled. "And get the hell out of here."

Bellamy didn't need to be told twice. He grabbed the case and rushed up to the cashier, practically throwing *renos* at the poor man before everything had been charged. He shoved the change back into his wallet, jostling it into his pocket frantically. Heads turned, watching him closely. Luckily, he made it outside and into the car before anyone bothered him. A ripple of need slammed into him as he closed the car's door.

Fuck.

He gripped the steering wheel with both hands, waiting for the wave of lust to die down a little. His cock tented his pants, the head leaking against the denim of his pants. When he finally got a little control over himself, he lifted his stare and saw the handsome alpha striding out of the store.

Where do I know him from?

The alpha was *so* familiar. Tall, dark, and handsome was an understatement. The guy had a full beard that could scratch his cheeks any day of the week. The alpha's broad shoulders filled his dress shirt well. Bellamy's stare moved down to the narrower waist… and then on to the tented tailored slacks. The imprint of the alpha's cock nearly took his breath away. Bellamy wanted to see it. *Feel* it. In his hands… between his lips… driving deep inside him.

A moan ripped from his lips, and he had to grasp the base of his own cock to prevent him from coming then and there on the spot.

The alpha paused, staring at Bellamy a moment—an odd look to his face. Bellamy held the man's gaze a few seconds before dragging his away, fearful much longer would push them into doing the unthinkable. Then and there in the parking lot. Up against a car without giving two shits who was watching. The image of that in his mind had another moan rising. He stared down at his hands… afraid what he might do next. It wasn't enough. He closed his eyes, willing himself to calm down.

Another wave of desire hit him as he saw himself writhing under the alpha… and he knew it was just his heat, fucking with his mind. He needed. *Badly.* Distance… he needed distance. And fast.

He turned the key and started the engine—but had to wait for the red sports car to back out and peel out of the parking lot before he could reverse. The same one he'd hit with his car door.

Oops…

The alpha was taking too damned long. When he looked into the rearview, he saw the man staring at the back of his head. Even from that distance, he could see the longing.

Could feel it bone deep.

Come on, come on, come on!

Bellamy reached for his phone as he waited, but changed his mind. It hadn't helped him much on the mountain roads—just as predicted. Digging into his pocket, he yanked out the map Tanner had drawn him.

Just get me there. Please. Before I lose my mind.

Finally, he heard the squealing of tires behind him. The little red sports car was gone—along with the hotter than fuck alpha driving it. Bellamy breathed a little easier and backed out, praying he'd make it to the lake house before the meds fully wore off.

****

Moments later...

Quinn jammed his foot on the accelerator, trying to put distance between him and the needy omega. His body still shook from the desire that had rocketed through him. The handsome omega's face was already burned into his brain, a seductive ghost still haunting him from miles away. Quinn wasn't sure how he'd had the strength to hold back... to let the omega go. Especially in his already stressed condition.

Why the hell the man was out in pubic in that condition was beyond him. There were meds that kept omegas out of heat and not in danger of being claimed publicly. Quinn had been seconds away from dragging the omega out of the store and bending him over the back of the car.

A rush of lust licked up his spine, the desire to turn the car around and do just that screaming in his veins. He'd forced himself into his own car and sped off—before he fucked up big time. That's all he needed.

As if his life wasn't a shitshow as it was.

By the time he reached the lake house gates, he'd cooled off substantially... though he was still sporting a semi-erection. He punched in the code at the gate and then watched as the metal bars slid out of his way. After pulling in, the gate closed again and he pulled his car into the garage. Quinn grabbed his overnight bag and the groceries he'd picked up before striding toward the back door and then into the kitchen.

After placing the few cold groceries into the fridge, he walked to the double doors leading out to the huge deck that went to the edge of the lake. Quinn hadn't been to the lake house in years, but it looked like nothing had changed outside it. The same houses surrounded the edges of the broad waters, little dots in the distance. On the far shore, the houses were more closely clustered versus the wide spreads of the houses on his family's side.

Quinn chuckled mirthlessly. His grandfather had likely spent a fortune on a house they never went to. He'd become too much like Tolliver. He worked his fingers to the bone and didn't spend any time appreciating the fruits of that labor.

The view here really is stunning. He walked out to gaze at the scenery and noticed the quiet. Exactly what he needed. He also saw the darkening sky above. Hints of a storm to come had hung above all through his trip, but now the darkness hinted at something dark and dangerous. He was thankful he'd made it before he'd gotten caught. It was almost as dark as night, the clouds heavy and pregnant with rain.

A burst of lightning illuminated the darkness seconds before the first fat drops hit the wood planks of the deck. The breeze scented of clean, fresh rain as it hit him in the face. Quinn slipped back inside just as the heavens opened and a torrent of rain slammed down upon the house.

He walked into the living room, and gazed around. All of the furniture was protected by dust covers and gave the place an eerie, ghostly appearance. With the thunder and pounding rain, he wondered if the trip hadn't been a mistake.

The gods only knew what Charles was doing at his house. Yet, if he'd stayed, he knew he might've ended up taking the beta back.

He was in the best spot he could be—miles from drama.

A chill raced down his spine. Quinn took it as a sign and started a fire in the gas hearth with the push of a button, hoping the flue had been cleaned as it should. A caretaker for the lake house lived not far, and maintained the property. It seemed the man was doing his job.

The fire roared to life. He stood back and let the warmth spread over him a moment, and made sure no black smoke filled the room, before returning to the kitchen and grabbing a bottle of beer. Once there, he frowned, really eyeing the refrigerator again. It looked as if it had been prepped for a visit.

Before a family visit, the caretaker would clean the place and fill the fridge with a few basics.

Was someone else coming up? *Dear gods, I hope not.*

He narrowed his eyes before reaching for his cell—only to remember he'd tossed it into the back of his car. Just as he was heading for the garage, he heard the front door opening. Quinn turned to see who'd arrived and began to walk out to the living room.

A drenched man stood in the doorway…

Heat slammed into Quinn, his dick re-hardening in an instant.

The guy pushed his wet hair from his forehead, and Quinn realized it wasn't just *any* guy.

One Wild Heat

It was the omega from the grocery.

The scent of the omega's slick immediately filled his nose again… his heart quickened… and the need to mate crashed into him.

Mine!

Chapter Three

Bellamy was soaking wet as he punched in the alarm code, as instructed—but instead of turning off, he somehow turned it on. *What the hell?* He punched the numbers in again, and the system deactivated. Frowning, he realized the house hadn't been secure before he walked in.

A sound came from somewhere in the house. Was there someone inside?

Oh shit.

A shiver raced down him, adding to the cold already seeping in. The storm had drenched him and hadn't shown signs of letting up. He'd raced out into it, hoping he wouldn't get soaked, but had failed miserably.

From the corner of his eye, he saw the flames in the fireplace. *Is someone here?* Another shiver raced down his spine...

Footsteps sounded behind him, and Bellamy spun, pushing his wet bangs from his forehead... just in time to see the alpha from the grocery standing just feet away. *What is he doing here?* The question was on his lips, but he couldn't get his mouth to work. Another wave of heat washed over him, making Bellamy's knees weak.

Silent tension filled the gap between them, and Bellamy felt both fear and desire unlike anything he'd ever experienced.

"What the hell are you doing here?" the alpha asked, his voice little more than a growl.

That was my question. The man's deep voice reverberated through him, sending his already lust-filled body over the edge. More of his slick eased out, spreading over his cheeks. He dropped to his knees, the need too overpowering.

Before he could answer, the alpha closed the gap, grabbed him, and pinned him to the floor. A firm set of lips pressed against his, knocking the air from his lungs. Bellamy kissed the stranger back with abandon, the animal need overriding his good sense. He could feel the hard ridge of the alpha's cock pressed against his stomach, and all he could think about was feeling it sliding into him. *Deep* into him.

"You shouldn't have come here," the alpha murmured against his lips. The man ground his hips against Bellamy, belying the words he spoke. "Not like this."

Bellamy undulated against him, writhing with lust. "Fuck me," he murmured against the alpha's lips. The innate need he felt had taken over. Now slave to his heat, he could only submit. "Please, alpha. Fuck me and fill me with your child."

The words sounded *so* foreign to his ears. Even his voice sounded strange. Of course he didn't want a stranger to put a child in him… but he was in full heat and the words were as instinctual as the lust he felt. It was all a part of the dance. A supplicant omega submitting to the powerful alpha's drive to procreate. It was how they were created.

It was also the reason there were drugs to stop moments like that…

A strong hand slid through his hair. His head was tugged back. The man trailed his heated lips up the column of Bellamy's neck, leaving a line of fire in its wake. "I'm going to fill you with my babe," the alpha growled once he reached Bellamy's lips. "Plant my seed deep, deep inside you."

Bellamy shook, the lust he felt too powerful to stop. His hands went to the alpha's belt and he unbuckled it with shaking hands. The sound of his shirt being ripped only made him shake all the harder. His wet clothes were rent from his body before he was carried toward the fireplace and laid on the thick rug there.

The alpha finished the job of opening his own pants. A thick, hard cock sprang free, and Bellamy moaned at the sight of it.

"I *need* you."

The alpha didn't hesitate. He grabbed the base of his shaft and pressed the head against Bellamy's soaked asshole. Yet the alpha held back, shaking as he knelt there, seconds from driving into Bellamy's body.

"*Please*," Bellamy begged, pleading for the relief only this alpha could give him.

The alpha drove hard, sliding halfway in before pausing. Bellamy moaned, the thick cock stretching him wide. It felt amazing, his ass gripping the shaft tight. The alpha thrust again, eliciting another moan. By the third thrust, he was fully seated, and Bellamy felt the pure delight of being filled to the hilt.

"My gods, you feel good wrapped around my cock," the alpha whispered thickly, pausing deep inside. He licked the inner shell of Bellamy's ear before he spoke again. "You're mine, little omega. *Mine.*"

Though the words were instinctual on the alpha's part, they did what they'd intended. Bellamy thrashed against the man, yearning to be bred.

"I can't wait to see your belly grow full with my babe," the alpha whispered before sliding out and driving back in.

Bellamy stared into the alpha's eyes, lost to the heat. "Give me what I need, alpha."

They writhed together on the thick rug, their bodies colliding in lust. On it went, what felt like hours. Sweat-coated and exhausted, they fucked before the roaring fire. Bellamy came over and over, screaming his release each time. Finally, he felt the alpha's body jerking and the swelling of the knot. The head of the alpha's cock slid into his womb, drawing a deep moan from him. Locked together, the alpha collapsed, pinning his weight on Bellamy.

"Can't… breathe…"

"Sorry," the alpha whispered, moving up to his elbows. He stared down at Bellamy, shadows flickering over his face from the fire. They both breathed hard for a moment, silent but for that sound.

Now that they'd both been sated, they had precious few moments of clarity before the next wave came. Locked together with a stranger, Bellamy didn't know what to say…

What *did* he say in a situation like that? He didn't even know the alpha's name.

"I never got that answer," the alpha whispered. "*Who* are you?"

"I'm a friend of the family who owns this house," Bellamy murmured between breaths. "And you?"

The alpha frowned. "A friend of the family? I *don't* know you."

Bellamy looked up and suddenly realized why the man looked familiar. "I'm a friend of Tanner's. He gave me the key and the security code. Said no one came up here, so I'd be okay." He offered a hand, realizing the ineptness of it considering the alpha's cock was still lodged deep inside him. "Bellamy."

Bellamy had a strong sensation the alpha above him was either Beau or Quinn. He hadn't met either of Tanner's alpha brothers yet… both were supposedly workaholics who moved in different crowds than their artistic younger brother.

What was a workaholic doing at a vacation house?

"I've never heard Tanner talk about a Bellamy…" the man said, narrowing his eyes.

Bellamy nearly moaned at the sound of his name on the alpha's lips. Another wave was coming… and quickly. "Tanner and I recently began sharing his studio space."

"Sharing his space?" Quinn asked, frowning. "I bought him that building. Why's he sharing it?"

Bellamy's eyes widened. Had he said something he shouldn't have? "There's an office downstairs… he rented it out to me a few months ago so I could start my business."

The alpha frowned again, staring down. He was silent a moment before shaking his head. "Maybe he did tell me. I vaguely recall him saying something about not wanting someone like me downstairs, so he'd found someone creative."

Bellamy nodded, chuckling. "He said he didn't want a stuffed shirt downstairs, so my business had the right energy and wouldn't oppress his art."

"His art," the alpha snapped, rolling his eyes. He took Bellamy's hand and held it tightly. "Quinn McCreary."

Oh fuck. While he'd already sensed the truth, hearing it confirmed only compounded the damage.

What if Tanner found out? What if he lost his office space? What would that do to his business?

"You shouldn't have come in this condition," Quinn murmured, huskily, breaking his downward spiral of dread. "What were you thinking?"

Bellamy frowned, anger swelling within him. "I was assured no one would be up here!"

"I nearly grabbed you at the store. It was filled with people. You shouldn't have been in there!"

"My heat came early," Bellamy spat. "The full moon hasn't even arrived. How was I to know?"

Quinn frowned. "Why aren't you on meds?"

"Leave it to the ignorant alpha to be unaware that omegas have to go off meds occasionally."

Quinn's face twisted in rage. "Did you just call me an ignorant alpha?"

"I did," Bellamy spat, angered that the man was making their situation to be all his fault.

Quinn growled, and the sound shot straight down Bellamy's spine. A moan bubbled up his chest.

"Don't *do* that."

"What? Don't get angry because some hippy, free-flying omega tricked me into fucking him?"

"Hippie, free-flying omega? Tricked? You asshole!"

Quinn tried to pull away, but the knot still joined them as one. Pulling at it only sent a tidal wave of need coursing through Bellamy. Another moan ripped from his throat. "My gods, *please…* stop pulling…"

"I didn't mean to hurt you," Quinn spat through clenched teeth.

"It *doesn't* hurt. Quite the opposite," Bellamy spat, glaring at the alpha.

Quinn paused, his mouth in an O, eyes filling with lust. "I didn't realize."

"Add it to the list of things Quinn McCreary doesn't comprehend."

Quinn narrowed his eyes again, and it pissed Bellamy off to no end that the man was substantially hotter when he was angry.

"What the hell do we do now?" Quinn asked.

Bellamy opened his mouth to answer, but the feel of Quinn against him was already beginning to prepare him for the next round. The need spread through his body and exited as another deep moan.

A growl rumbled up Quinn's chest, and the sound sent a wave of slick dribbling from him. Bellamy stretched slightly, and again the knot pulled against him. Another moan fell from his lips. They hadn't even finished one round of fucking and he was already growing greedy for another. Three years of putting things off had been a mistake. "As soon as the knot fades… leave. As fast as you can."

"It's my family's lake house. Why should I go?"

"I'm in no condition to go right now!" Bellamy cried. "You need to leave, alpha!"

Lightning filled the room, thunder shaking the very house around them.

"I don't think it's safe for either of us to leave," Quinn said, his voice growing huskier. "Yet it's not safe for us both to be here, is it?" He moved again, pulling against the knot. Quinn lifted his hand and spread his hand through the hair at the back of Bellamy's head. He knotted his fingers, tugging.

The heat returned in a massive wave, making them both forget the arguments of moments ago. They both moaned before their lips met, both hungry for the kiss that came. When they parted, they both struggled to breathe. Bellamy's need was feeding Quinn's. As his heat built, the alpha's need to rut grew.

They would continue to feed off one another for days if one of them didn't escape.

"I don't think we're making it out of this house," Quinn whispered before trailing his lips down Bellamy's throat. "Not until your heat has run its course."

Bellamy closed his eyes, the feel of the alpha's lips on his skin like fire. His slick leaked heavily from him at that point, coating his ass with plenty of natural lubricant. As the knot faded, a still hard shaft filled him.

Condom. Tell him to put on a condom. The words whispered through Bellamy's mind, but never fell from his lips.

Quinn moved into position, ready to continue the dance they'd already begun.

"Fill me, alpha." The words came pouring from Bellamy's lips, untethered, without the precaution slipping through.

"Anything you wish, my omega."

Bellamy moaned loudly as Quinn drew him up. Seated in the alpha's lap, he bore down on the thick cock spearing into him. Molten, he leaned into Quinn... his body and lips begging for more.

****

Many hours later...

Quinn's eyes opened. He stared up at the ceiling, momentarily forgetting where he was. It took a few seconds. Looking over the warm body of the omega cuddled up against him helped bring him back to the present. Bellamy's head rested on his shoulder, sleep having claimed the man. Quinn lifted a hand to brush back a little of the guy's too long bangs and got his first really good look at the omega.

He's perfect.

Long, dark lashes swept over chiseled cheekbones, just a bit more ebony than his hair and brows. A day's worth of beard growth dotted his cheeks, but didn't hide how soft and smooth his skin was. His skin was lightly tanned with a few freckles peeking out. Quinn's gazed swept down to the full lips that begged to be kissed. Bellamy's eyes were golden. The fire had almost made them look as if they were aflame. Quinn was fairly sure he could look at those eyes for the rest of his life.

Quinn closed his own eyes, realizing the insanity of that contemplation.

What have I done?

This wasn't the way he'd expected his weekend to go—running from the end of a bad relationship and spending a night having wild, animalistic sex with another man. A stranger. *Yet not a stranger, if he's mine.*

Quinn had never experienced full rut, and his body was sore all over. One night and he was already exhausted.

There were three more to come…

After five rounds of sex on the floor—at least he thought it had been five, the hours had merged together after a certain point—they'd fallen asleep before the fireplace. Quinn carefully extracted himself from where Bellamy lay and dragged himself to his feet. He made his way to the kitchen and grabbed a bottle of water. Draining it in one long gulp, he then grabbed another two bottles and walked back to the living room.

Outside was barely gray. The fire had long died out, and now there was a chill in the room. He worried about his omega. They had little time to spare before the next wave came. Quinn knelt beside Bellamy and opened one of the bottles before lifting the omega's head and tilting the bottle close. "Drink, baby."

Bellamy's eyes flickered open and then closed before he took a few drinks. His eyes opened again and his hand took over the bottle, lifting it to drain the contents. He handed the bottle back to Quinn.

"More," Bellamy cried, his voice hoarse from all the cries of pleasure that had ripped from him over the night.

Quinn had another ready and opened it before handing it to the omega. Bellamy drained half of the bottle before lowering it and sighing. "Thank you."

He took the bottle from Bellamy and drank the rest of it. "We can't get dehydrated." It was then that he remembered the omega reaching for the case of water. He saw it beside the bags still left just inside the door.

Quinn quickly lifted Bellamy in his arms.

"What're you doing?"

"Taking you somewhere more comfortable while we have time," Quinn murmured, knowing their time was brief.

Bellamy struggled in his arms. "I can walk."

Quinn clenched him tighter, drawing the naked man closer. "Stop," he growled. Even the little moment of fighting turned him on.

Bellamy looked up at him, those golden eyes bright with lust.

"Let me take you to bed," Quinn said, his voice growing deeper to his own ears.

The omega's eyes narrowed, and Quinn was fairly sure the man was about to argue with him again. The thought brought a smile to his lips… he happily anticipated the spark of anger in the omega. Quinn nearly dropped the man then and there to take him again. Instead, he rushed into the first-floor master suite. After depositing Bellamy into a covered chair, he stripped the dust cover from the huge bed and checked for sheets. Luckily, the bed was made underneath.

Spinning, he eyed Bellamy and felt another wave of heat hit. "Get in," he growled before pointing back out to the living room. "Water."

Bellamy nodded. "Meal bars… in the bag…"

Quinn struggled to leave Bellamy. He heard the panting need in the omega's voice. After collecting the case of water, the box of meal bars, and Bellamy's bag, he returned to the bedroom and deposited them all beside the chair. He stalked to the end of the bed and eyed the man, writhing in the sheets.

Bellamy lay there, stroking his hard cock and moaning. Quinn bit the inside of his cheek, delighted to watch the show before him a moment longer. His hands fisted at his sides as he watched Bellamy's pleasure, wanting to be the one to give it.

Mine.

The word whispered in his mind again, unsettling him.

What in the hell are we doing? We're practically strangers…

Bellamy's moan flipped a switch in Quinn's mind. All wayward thoughts faded in an instant. A growl rose up Quinn's throat before he slid into the bed and pinned his omega below him.

And then he proceeded to fuck Bellamy six ways from Sunday.

Chapter Four

A couple of days or so later…

Bellamy rolled over late in the morning, his body aching. He'd lost track of how many times they'd fucked. Hell, he'd lost track of what day it was. Thinking back, he wasn't completely sure if it had been two days… or three.

Please gods, don't make this last much longer.

It had been so long since he'd been in heat, without any meds to block it, and he'd forgotten just how overpowering it was. The last time had been a decade before. At seventeen, when he'd had it the first time. Just like then, he was a slave to instinct, his body overriding his mind.

Only this time, he'd dragged another into the chaos.

He glanced at the snoozing alpha lying beside him. Half of Quinn's face was buried in the twisted sheets they'd half ripped from the bed in their lust for one another. The other half showed just how handsome Quinn McCreary was.

Dark haired. Dark eyed. Tanned skin, although as much as the man supposedly worked, he didn't know how Quinn found time for sun. He did look much like Tanner, just in a bigger, harder, more masculine way.

Handsome. And good in bed. That was about where Bellamy ended the list of qualities.

Quinn was dominating. Argumentative. Had to have his way—which Bellamy wanted to put on the good side of the list because it was turning him the hell on, but the liberal, independent omega side of him demanded it go on the negative side.

Of course, the only time he'd spent with Quinn was a few days in bed, ensorcelled by an instinctual need that ruled them all.

So why am I so drawn to him?

Bellamy moved a hand and brushed some of Quinn's bangs from his forehead. *He really is handsome.*

He felt an electric arc of need shoot through him from his fingertips barely grazing over the man's hair. A moan tore from his lips, and he felt the need wash through him once more. Not again.

The alpha's eyes popped open. Quinn was up and on top of Bellamy in an instant, smothering him with kisses. Kisses Bellamy was already growing quite addicted to. His tongue warred with Quinn's… tasting… tempting…

It didn't take long for Quinn to slide back inside Bellamy's slickened ass, and they moved in concert, writhing and twisting in the sheets again.

Bellamy looked up at the alpha, pinned by the look in the man's eyes.

Mine.

Bellamy gasped at the word whispered in his mind. *No, no, no…*

It's just the wild heat. Four years of lust building up in my system. He's not mine…

Yet why did he close his eyes and pretend for a moment that Quinn was?

****

Quinn glanced down at the omega, his heart beating fiercely as they came together, over and over. While it had only been a few days, it felt as if they'd known each other forever. They moved together as if they'd performed this dance before, years of practiced carnality. Bellamy's body felt made for his…

And a little part of him pretended that this omega *was* his.

This is what it would feel like to be bound.

To begin a family.

A legacy.

He slid his hand through Bellamy's hair and tugged, forcing the omega to look up at him as he thrust deep. Quinn felt in those moments, he could look down at Bellamy for the rest of his life. That he *wanted* to look down at Bellamy for the rest of his life.

Which was insane.

It's just the rut. The instinct. Nothing more.
It'll all be over soon.

Yet, he didn't want it to be over. Not even close.

****

Four days turned into five. Bellamy had waited much too long, and now he was being punished for it. By the end of those five days, Bellamy's body was utterly exhausted. He lay boneless on the bed, partially draped over Quinn's body, both of them rapidly breathing.

Oh gods, please let it be over.

Not that Quinn wasn't an impressive lover—because he'd been *amazing*—but five non-stop days of *anything* was too much. Bellamy ached in places he'd forgotten he had. He was starving. Dying of thirst. He wanted to sleep for a month. Or maybe take a three-hour-long shower. Yet, the thought of moving didn't sound particularly appealing, either.

Maybe I'll just die here on the spot.

"Do you think we're finally done?" Quinn whispered against his forehead before pressing a kiss there.

"Possibly," Bellamy said. Even though he was happy to be done, the thought of Quinn walking away after their long weekend was enough to make him stop breathing. *It's just the aftereffects of a full heat. He means nothing to me.*

Nothing.

Bellamy frowned, knowing that wasn't true. Even if they'd come together as strangers, after their days shared, they both knew one another in ways most never would. Both had seen the other's latent desires, their animal need. Not even Fritz had seen Bellamy in such a state.

They lay there for the better part of an hour, silent. Waiting to see if another wave of desire would enslave them. Finally, Quinn rolled to his side and smirked. "I think we're in the clear."

Bellamy nodded, forcing a smile. Now what happened? Would the alpha run for the hills, leaving him there alone?

I would in his shoes. He didn't want this. No more than I did.

Quinn quickly slid from the bed and marched into the bathroom.

Couldn't get away from me fast enough. Bellamy winced, wondering why he'd think that. Quinn owed him nothing. To expect anything from the alpha was presumptuous, at best.

Still, it stung.

Bellamy tried to roll himself to the edge but struggled to move. Every muscle in his body ached. Finally, he got himself seated at the side of the bed, both feet squarely on the cool, wooden floor. He stared around at the bedroom, really seeing it for the first time in days. Everything was white. White walls. White drapes. White bedding. A couple of paintings graced the walls, both with pale pastel shades that did nothing to add life to the room.

Of course, he'd seen these things all along, yet hadn't really seen them. Nothing had mattered except for the sensation of the alpha driving deep within him.

He'd been too focused on touch. Taste. *Feel.*

A tremor raced up Bellamy's body, and he felt a whispered touch along his skin. He looked over his shoulder, almost sure Quinn was behind him—only to see no one was there. A mild wave of heat washed over him—nothing like the desire that had crashed over and over, breaking him—but a mini aftershock. He held back the moan in the back of his throat and refused to call for Quinn to return to him and sate that one last glimmer of lust.

He stared down at the pale gray wooden floor, cringing. The place was devoid of color. Of soul. He barely remembered what he'd seen as he'd first come in, but he thought it had been slip-covers. More white.

The lake house, while beautiful, was bland as hell.

What I could do with a place like this…

The sound of water rushing filled the bathroom behind him.

Suddenly, Quinn was in front of him, kneeling. "Sore?"

Bellamy nodded, holding his breath slightly. He stared down at the most handsome man he'd ever seen. Lust of a different kind spread through him, and he fought it off.

"I'm running you a bath now. Should help make you feel a little better."

A chemical in the alpha brain triggered at the end of a heat, one that urged the male to comfort his omega. Quinn was still a slave to Bellamy's heat, trapped in this need to protect and soothe. "You don't have to do that…"

Quinn cupped his cheek and lifted his stare slightly. "Of course I do."

Bellamy stared at the loving look in Quinn's eyes and froze. His stomach clenched. "You know this is just the aftereffects of the heat. What you're feeling now?"

"I know," Quinn murmured, smiling slightly. "Of course, even without it, I would tend to my mate."

Bellamy's eyes rounded in horror. "Mate?" Quinn leaned in and attempted to kiss him. Bellamy pulled away. "Hold on, alpha. It's just the lingering effects from the heat… from me having waited so long between med breaks. We're *not* mates. It was a wild heat—stronger than a normal heat." Suddenly, Bellamy was lifted in the strong alpha's arms… again. "Like I said the last time… I can walk."

"Okay," Quinn replied before lowering Bellamy's feet to the floor.

Bellamy grabbed ahold of Quinn's arms, unsteady. He tried to take a few tentative steps and hissed in pain before being swept back into Quinn's arms.

"It'll be easier this way," Quinn murmured before carrying him to the bath.

He wanted to argue, but it was hard when he knew Quinn wasn't himself. Perhaps it was just easier to let it runs its course. The alpha lowered him into the warm bath, and he moaned with delight as he rested under the warmth. His muscles immediately relaxed some. "That feels *sooo* good."

Quinn produced a washcloth and lowered it with one hand into the water. "I need to wash you. Once I'm done, you can relax while I change the sheets. You'll need some rest after our days together." He lifted his stare. "Do you need me to fix you something to eat?"

My gods, it's like it's not even him. The afterglow… Bellamy had never seen an alpha like this, and it was strange. And easy to get wrapped up in. "No… I can grab one of the meal bars I brought."

"You need more than that, I'm sure," Quinn replied, trailing a strong hand and the washcloth down his leg.

Bellamy looked up into the man's handsome face, wanting to melt into the water and give in to the alpha's tending. It would be so easy to, but also unfair. What they felt wasn't real. They weren't bond-mates, no matter how much it felt like they were. And Quinn had to be just as exhausted as he was. "I'm sorry."

Quinn paused, frowning. "Sorry? For what?"

"For being here… like this… had I known you were here…" Bellamy paused, shaking his head. "I wouldn't have come had I known."

Quinn's hand stopped. "Look… we were put into an untenable situation and things happened." He smiled softly. "You're my bond-mate… and whatever happened was simply fate bringing us together."

"I feel the pull to you, too. I do. But I think it's me causing it. I took too long between breaks and I went into a wild heat. They're dangerous. I know they can play tricks on omega minds and bodies… I assume it might do the same for alphas, too."

One of Quinn's brows rose. "A wild heat?"

Bellamy took a deep breath. Most alphas knew so little about omegas and reproduction. "Omegas are supposed to go off meds one month a year… to help their systems regulate. *Heatex* is harsh on us. Our systems were meant to go into heat every month, and holding back the tide has repercussions. I've pushed things… it's been about four years since I last went off meds… so this was *way* past due. And likely why I went into heat early. It wasn't supposed to start until the night after I got here."

Quinn blew out a heavy breath. "The meds affect you, not me. What I feel is true."

"Quinn, I didn't stop taking the scent blocker."

The alpha frowned, and Bellamy sighed again.

"Unmated omegas take *two* meds. One stops our heats—*Heatex*—another blocks our scent—*Scentex*—together, they prevent us from being claimed by *any* alpha—our mate or otherwise. It's what allows us to be free… to go wherever we want and not be locked away as they did in the past." He paused seeing the sappy, romantic look on Quinn's face diminishing. The more time that passed, the more Quinn would see reason. The afterglow would fade… leaving them with only the truth. "I only stopped the heat blocker. *Not* the scent blocker. There's no way you could know I'm *anything* to you."

Quinn rested back on his heels and eyed him.

"Trust me, I feel it, too. I feel the bond and the pull toward you—but it's just the lingering heat messing with our minds and bodies. It'll pass. And we'll be free of one another."

Quinn was quiet for a moment before he tossed the washcloth onto the edge of the bathtub. "What if I don't want to be free of this?"

Bellamy gasped inwardly, his heartbeat growing rapid. He held Quinn's heated stare for a moment before pulling it away. "Leave, Quinn. Before we say or do things we'll regret. Once the smoke clears, we'll feel foolish for even thinking it."

"What would I regret?" Quinn asked, his hand snaking up Bellamy's leg. "I want you, omega."

Bellamy pushed the alpha's hand away harshly, trying to save them both. "Get out! *Please.*"

Quinn stared at him, frowning. "You don't mean that."

"I don't want you in here. I need to be alone," Bellamy said, allowing his voice to grow harsh. The alpha had done nothing wrong, and didn't deserve his ire—but he had to save them both from making things any worse than they already were.

Quinn blinked a few times before rising to his full height. He stared down at Bellamy in the tub a moment before his face twisted in anger. "I sure as hell wouldn't have come here had I known I'd end up forced into a situation with a jerk like you."

"Tanner said he would call everyone," Bellamy murmured. "I assumed he had. The last thing I wanted was to walk in on an alpha when I was in heat. A perfect stranger, at that." Bellamy turned his stare away. "Now we can go back to being strangers. Forget any of this even happened."

"Forget?" Quinn chuckled mirthlessly before all the light disappeared from his eyes. "Fine. You want to forget it, so be it."

"Trust me. You'll be glad I sent you away when this is all over."

Bellamy could feel Quinn's stare on him, but forced himself not to look. After a moment, the alpha stormed out and left him alone.

Just as he'd demanded.

Bellamy sank a little deeper under the water and sighed, his body still yearning to be close to Quinn's.

He's not mine.

Let him go.

Yet his body wouldn't listen. He could still feel Quinn's hands, lips, and thick shaft on and inside him.

He felt marked by the man… and he wasn't sure there was enough soap in the province to wash it away.

****

Twenty-four hours later…

Quinn laid his go-bag into the trunk of his car, still feeling odd about simply leaving without… *anything…*

It's what he wanted. He said so himself. Forget.

He'd heard little from Bellamy over the last day, besides the occasional sound of footsteps and an occasional snore as he pressed an ear to the door. While Quinn had wanted nothing better than to immediately put distance between them, five days of sex had left him dehydrated and running on empty.

After devouring most of the food he'd brought with him, he'd slept for hours. Later, he'd awoken, showered, and re-packed what little he'd used before escaping to the garage—bag in hand.

Lifting his stare, he eyed the door he'd just exited, wondering if he should say his goodbyes. But the thought of facing the omega again left him feeling strange. *Two strangers forced together…*

He ached to see Bellamy again, but the omega's words whispered in his mind.

It's just the aftereffects…

We go back to being strangers…

Strangers.

They weren't strangers. Not anymore. Never would be, no matter how much they tried.

Quinn had come for peace and quiet and got none of that. It was better to just break away and put it in his past, just as Bellamy had suggested. Pretend it didn't happen.

He slid in behind the wheel of his car before reversing out of the garage. As soon as he was outside the gates and roaring down the mountain road, he sensed his mistake.

Quinn wanted to turn the car around and return to his omega.

He's not *my omega. He said so himself. Go home.*

Trying to ignore the question whispering on the frayed edges of his mind, Quinn stamped on the accelerator and raced toward home.

But that question plagued him the whole way.

What if he's carrying my child?

****

Bellamy stood at the window, watching the little red sports car rip out of the lake house's drive. He felt an ache in his chest as it disappeared from view. A little sob rose up his throat, and he shook his head at his own absurdity. "Quinn McCreary is *not* for me."

Then why does him leaving without saying goodbye hurt so motherfucking bad?

He walked over to where his bag rested and fished out his cellphone. Thirty-six missed calls?

Two were from friends. Three were from Tanner. The rest were all Fitz. He sighed, almost wishing he *had* brought Fitz with him.

No. That just would've made things worse.

He hit the messages from Tanner first.

Hey, B! Look, I just heard through the grapevine my older brother Quinn might be heading your way. I called him and left a message, but Mr. High and Mighty barely listens to me, so who knows if he paid any attention. I've asked Beau to call him, too, but if he gets there—just tell him to call me. I hope you have a good weekend, darling!

Bellamy clicked off the message. *Well, that got to me too late. Not that telling Quinn would've done any good.* He clicked on the second message.

Tanner sounded a little more panicked. *Hey B. I couldn't get through to Quinn and neither could Beau. I'm hoping you're okay and he got the message and hightailed it somewhere else. Call me as soon as you can and let me know you're okay. I feel terrible. I promised you'd be safe and hopefully I didn't turn out to be a liar. So… just call, me 'kay?*

Bellamy clicked off the second message and went to the third.

So, I'm assuming at this point my brother is balls deep… wait, no, I really don't want that image seared into my noggin. Forget I said it. Rewind and begin again. Just… I don't know… call me when you can so I know you're okay. I'm worried about you. I need to know you're okay. Love ya.

Bellamy stared down at the phone after lowering it. He wasn't in the mood to discuss what happened, but he didn't want Tanner to continue worrying. And then there were the twenty messages from Fitz, which he really didn't feel like wading through at that point, either. After considering a moment, he lifted the phone and typed out a text, sending it to them both.

I'm okay. Heading home in a few minutes. See you soon!

After hitting Send, he stared at the screen and saw two message bubbles pop up. Quickly turning off his phone, he tucked it into his bag before rising. Bellamy wasn't going to sit there for an hour typing answers to the million questions to come regarding his long weekend. He pulled the bag's strap across his body and gazed around at the lake house one last time.

The fireplace caught his attention. And the thick rug lying before it.

He'd never forget that first night. It was seared into his memory.

Chapter Five

Back home…

Quinn pulled through the gates at his cliff-side home and drove on toward the towering house. The modern structure—all metal and glass—was quite opposite the lake house and a jarring reminder that he was back to reality. Another jarring reminder he'd been dragged from a dream was Charles' car parked before the house.

I'm not ready for this.

As he climbed out of the little red coupe, Charles came rushing down the front stairs, tears streaming down his face. "You're alive! Oh, thank the gods!"

The beta slammed into him, wrapping him in a tight hug. "I was so worried, Quinn. I thought you'd had an accident. I've been calling you for days."

Quinn extracted himself from Charles' hold. Had Beau let him stay? "I said you needed to be gone when I got back. Why are you here?"

Charles frowned. "I knew once you cooled off, you'd be fine. But then you didn't come home…" The waterworks began again. "And I was terrified something had happened. You said you'd be gone the weekend and it's been six days, Quinn. No word. No *anything.*" Charles punched his arm. "How could you? Was this some kind of punishment?"

Quinn stared down at the beta, confused. "You're not going to worm your way back in this time."

"We're too good for one another for this to be over," Charles said, tilting his head with a smile to his lips. "You must realize that."

"No… we're *not* good for one another," Quinn said, too exhausted to continue this argument over and over.

"We have similar friends… similar interests… we grew up in the same world, Quinn. Together, we're stronger."

The words sounded so familiar to the ones his grandfather had said just a week before. Who was coaching who? Had the mating idea even been his grandfather's… or was it Charles'?

"I mean *nothing* to you… besides my money and social standing. And the chances you might bag yourself an alpha." He smiled, suddenly realizing the truth to that statement. "That's it, isn't it? You want to be able to say you got an alpha, even though you're only a beta."

Charles' face twisted in anger before he took a step back. "Now you're just being cruel."

"Cruel?" Quinn chuckled. "I hit the nail on the head, didn't I?"

Charles scowled, but remained silent.

"Pack your shit and get out, Charles. Or I'll call the guard to come drag you out of here, kicking and screaming if I have to."

Charles froze, his eyes widening. "You've got to be kidding me…"

"I'm not." He stalked into the house and toward their bedroom, Charles in pursuit behind him. Once inside the big closet in their room, he snagged one of Charles' suitcases and came out, tossing it on the bed. "Here. Let me help you."

He returned to the closet, gathering up an armload of suits before returning to toss them beside the suitcase. "Get packing."

"Quinn… get real. You're not throwing me out."

"I did. Six days ago. You should be gone by now."

Charles stalked closer, snaking his arms around Quinn. "Let's talk this out… there has to be a way to find our way back to when things were good."

"They haven't been good for months and you know it. We might as well be strangers." Quinn jerked at the mention of strangers… he felt closer to Bellamy after a week than he did with the man he'd lived with for nearly two years.

"And what about my father? You know he's ill. You'll just abandon me in my time of need?"

"Don't use his illness to stick your claws back into me," Quinn spat.

"You're a monster!"

Quinn sighed. "I'm sorry about your father. I am, but this should've been over a long time ago. You know it as well as I do. Now you can focus on your father's health. Be there for your parents in their time of need. Forget about me. All I want to do is forget about you."

Charles stared at him, looking dumbfounded. Anger twisted over his face, and he lifted his chin haughtily. He tossed a few more things into the suitcase before locking it and snatching it off the bed. "I'll send someone to pack the rest of my things."

The beta stormed out. Quinn followed a little farther behind, just to make sure the man did indeed leave, but when he saw Charles in the back of his red coupe, he rushed out.

"What're you doing?" Quinn asked as he moved to the driver's door.

Charles lifted a hand, an old pair of sunglasses in his grasp. "I left these in the back the last time we had a road trip. I didn't want to forget them."

The beta spun and walked over to his own car, his head held high. He slid in behind the wheel and soon raced off. Quinn watched until Charles' car couldn't be seen any longer—and felt a weight lifted off his shoulders.

Before going back inside, Quinn grabbed his go-bag from the trunk—and then remembered his cell phone. He rooted around in the backseat, but couldn't find it. After searching under the seats and pulling everything out that he could, he sat back and remembered Charles in his car, reaching for something.

What reason would he have to take my phone?

Other than to piss me off?

Whatever. He won't be able to hack it. I'll just get a new one.

Quinn growled. Either way, the loss of his phone was a big deal. His schedule, his work contacts, his friends' numbers… it was all there. He gave the car one more look before giving up the search. Once inside, he called the phone company from his home phone to have it shut down… and to order a new one to be couriered to his office the next day.

He then collapsed on the couch, exhausted. The view of the valley below was stunning—yet all he could see in his mind was his omega.

Not my *omega.*

Heat slammed into him, his cock growing hard. He closed his eyes and all he saw was Bellamy writhing and pleading under him.

Fill me, alpha.

After unzipping, he reached into his pants and stroked the length of his cock, circling the head on the upswing and spreading his pre-cum over the head. He quickened his pace, imagining it was the omega's hand and not his own. He let out a few pants and groans as he worked his flesh, pushing himself to the edge.

He came, almost soundlessly. Cum filled his hands and spread down the length of his cock. He looked down at the mess he'd made, indifferent. It hadn't been enough to truly sate him. Only Bellamy's mouth, hands, and body could do that for him.

Quinn was already obsessed with the man. He wondered if he'd ever have enough time and space between them for it to wear off.

Doubtful.

****

Later that evening…

The sun had just set when Bellamy pulled up to his rented brownstone and shifted the borrowed car into park. Before he exited, he rested there a moment, feeling wearier than he could ever recall. It was finally over, and now his life could return to some semblance of normalcy—though he wasn't sure he'd ever feel normal again. His body was sore. His soul was weary.

And all he wanted to do was go back and live through it all over again.

He could still feel Quinn's hands on him. Quinn's lips. Quinn's strong body pinning him down. A shiver raced up his spine, with a hint of need sparking in his blood.

A few drops of rain landed on his windshield. It spurred him into action. He jumped out of the car and grabbed his bags before a deluge came. As soon as he'd closed the trunk, he saw he had visitors waiting on his stoop. Eyeing Fitz and Tanner seated on the steps, he knew the quiet evening at home he'd imagined was rapidly going up in smoke.

He came to a stop at the base of the stairs and stared at the pair—who were for once in close proximity and *not* arguing. They were silent, appraising him closely, as if they could determine what had happened in a single sweep of the gaze. Fitz drew in a deep breath before frowning deeply, his jaw setting into a firm line.

Finally, Tanner jumped up and raced down the three steps to wrap his arms around Bellamy. "Thanks the gods you're home! I was so worried."

The loose droplets of rain started coming down a little harder. "Can we go inside so I don't end up like a drowned rat for the second time in a week?"

Fitz rose silently and let Bellamy ascend. He opened the door and felt the pair slip in behind him, carefully stepping over the piles of mail awaiting his perusal. Bellamy laid his bag on the bottom step of the staircase to the right as his friends moved into the living room. He scooped up the mail, searching through it once collected, looking for anything of importance. Anything to stave off the questions he knew were coming.

"You don't have to ignore us," Fitz called across the room. "I can smell another alpha on you. Doesn't take a genius to fill in the blanks."

Tense silence filled the space as Bellamy lifted his head and stared at Fitz. His attention then went to a wide-eyed Tanner.

"Quinn?" Tanner asked, his normally jubilant voice much lower and calmer in tone.

Bellamy didn't owe either of them any explanation. He was a grown man. His love life was his own, yet he couldn't stop the torrent of words that had been circling through his mind the entire trip home. "It had been too long since I cycled off. I went into heat early… a wild heat, I think… and Quinn was there. We couldn't fight the instinct. It… just happened."

"A wild heat?" Tanner asked before whistling lowly. "I've heard they can be horrendous."

Fitz growled. "Had I been there—"

Bellamy lifted a hand, silencing Fitz. "We both know it was best you weren't."

Tanner looked between them, frowning. "Why was it best Fitz wasn't there? I mean… I thought he's your man?"

Bellamy's face grew redder. "I'm really not in the mood to go point by point in my love life and explain who, what, why, and when I choose to do anything."

"I wasn't judging," Tanner said, flopping down on the couch. "I just thought you two kinda had a thing."

"We do," Fitz spat.

"Yes, but…" Bellamy shook his head and lifted his stare to Fitz. "That's for a private conversation."

Awkward silence filled the room.

"Once again, I feel the cue for me to leave. Keep it up and I might start getting a complex," Tanner said before hopping off the couch. He gave one last pointed look at Fitz before turning to Bellamy. "I want more deets…" Tanner pointed to Bellamy's stomach. "Especially if you might be carrying my nephew in there."

Fitz growled, and it only made Tanner smile even more. His friend walked closer on his way toward the door and paused inches before Bellamy.

"*Are* you okay?" Tanner whispered, the smile faded.

"I am." *I will be. Hopefully.*

"He didn't hurt you, did he? Because I'll have his head if he did."

Bellamy chuckled. "He didn't hurt me. Not at all." *He was considerate, even at the height of my need. He was exactly what I needed.*

The thought rocked through him. Bellamy had thought, wrong place, wrong time, but maybe it hadn't been that after all. Would he have been able to suffer through a wild heat alone? Or would he have climbed the walls and gone in search of an alpha… *any* alpha… to ease the ache within? Maybe he should be glad Quinn had been there when he'd walked in. Another might not have been so kind to him.

Tanner glanced down and then lifted his stare. "Might there be a mini McCreary in there? Or did you actually have the presence of mind to remember condoms?"

"I didn't think I was going to face an alpha… so I didn't bring any… nor did I have the wherewithal to even ask." Bellamy sighed. "I forgot how intense a heat is… and with an alpha there… it felt even stronger than what I remember."

"With a wild heat, I doubt you did," Tanner murmured. "But figured I'd ask if you'd been protected."

"I suppose fate will have its way with me."

Tanner leaned in for a hug and whispered in his ear. "You know how to reach me if you need anything. I'm here for you, for *anything*, B."

"Thanks," Bellamy whispered in reply.

Tanner stepped back, turned slightly to salute Fitz with a middle finger, and then was off, leaving the pair of them alone. Fitz was silent a few minutes and honestly, Bellamy wasn't sure he was ready for whatever was going to come out of the alpha's mouth.

"I know you don't feel for me what I feel for you. You owe me nothing," Fitz said. "But this hurts. Knowing another alpha was there in *my* place. I won't lie and say it doesn't."

"But it wasn't your place, Fitz." He paused as he saw a fresh wave of hurt wash over the man's face. "I would never do anything to purposely hurt you. You *know* that. It simply… *happened*. It wasn't planned. It was…" *Fate? No. Not fate.* "An accident."

Fitz was silent another moment. "What happens if you're *accidentally* pregnant?"

Bellamy shrugged. "I honestly don't know." He wasn't ready to carry a child. He'd just opened his own business and was doing well for himself, but things were still hard. He still worried about making enough to pay his rent each month. So far, he'd been lucky. But what happened next month? Or the one after?

Fitz moved in close. "If that McCreary bastard doesn't step up… you know I will."

Bellamy gasped. "I couldn't ask you to do that."

"I love you."

Bellamy's heart ached. "It would be selfish of me to do that. I won't rob you of your own forever."

Fitz closed the gap between them and gathered Bellamy's chin in one hand. "*You* make me happy."

Bellamy frowned. "I'm *not* your bond-mate."

"I don't care!"

Bellamy opened his mouth to argue, but Fitz swept in and covered his mouth with a kiss. For the first time, it felt wrong.

Really, *really* wrong.

Bellamy pushed him away, an image of Quinn coming to his mind. His head swam as a realization began to sweep over him.

Oh gods.

Maybe he is mine.

Quinn McCreary? My bond-mate?

As he stared down, Fitz looked as confused as Bellamy felt. The alpha took a step back, anger in his eyes.

"I can see you want to be alone," Fitz barked before heading for the door. He nearly slammed it on his way out.

Bellamy stood there, frozen.

What the hell do I do now?

One Wild Heat

Chapter Six

Early the following morning…

When Quinn strode into McCreary Towers, only the janitorial staff were there, polishing the marble floors of the lobby. They paid him little attention as he stalked up to one of the elevators and punched the button. Quinn was often the first to enter the building in the mornings and often the last to leave—which only made his sudden disappearance likely stand out all the more.

He was ready to get back to the world he knew, and didn't want to have all eyes on him as he walked in. Nor was he prepared to answer questions about his absence, though he knew he would have to come up with something eventually. After an hour or so, he'd sorted through messages on his desk before sitting down to check his emails. Halfway through and unable to focus, he spun in his chair and looked down at the awakening city. The sun was just rising, casting a golden glow outside his window. Skyscrapers clad in glass and metal shone with the light of the sun, making it look as if the whole city was on fire.

Turning his gaze down, he saw dozens of men walked along the sidewalks below, looking like ants from his great height.

Are you down there somewhere, Bellamy?

Quinn felt his heartbeat quicken a little just at the thought of running into the omega again.

"There you are!" Beau cried from behind him, bursting into the office. Quinn spun his chair to face his younger brother. "I'm so glad to finally see you back. You had us all worried."

"Yes," he smiled slightly. "I'm back." *Though I wish I was still in bed with my omega.*

My omega? He's not mine. He said so himself.

"Where did you go?" Beau asked.

Quinn frowned. His brother knew exactly where he'd gone.

Beau's face went ashen. "Please tell me you got our messages and went somewhere else."

Quinn frown grew deeper. *The phone. What else have I missed?* "I'm afraid my phone was destroyed while I was away. I've got another ordered, and it should be delivered here shortly."

"I don't care much about your phone. I'm more worried about the omega," Beau said, his brows slanting even farther down.

"You know about that, hmm?"

"Just after you left, Tanner called me. He'd forgotten to tell us he'd offered the lake house to an omega friend who was going off-meds this weekend. *Off-meds*," Beau repeated, emphasizing the latter. "We both called you. Numerous times… and you never answered."

Quinn stiffened. "Like I said… my phone was damaged."

"You… didn't… *get stuck*… did you?"

Quinn forced a smile. "No worries," he answered, avoiding an actual answer.

"Good," Beau said, looking relieved. He sat down in the chair opposite the desk. "Where *did* you go?"

"Somewhere where I didn't think about work once," Quinn answered honestly. For the first time in over a decade, work hadn't come to his mind while he'd been in bed with Bellamy. "And now it's back to the grind."

Beau smiled his way.

"By the way… Charles was waiting for me when I returned. All his stuff was still in my house. What the hell happened?"

Beau grinned painfully and was just about to answer when they were interrupted.

Quinn's assistant knocked on the door and peeked inside. "Good morning, Mr. McCreary. I'm glad to see you."

"And you, as well, Peter."

"I have more messages for you, but before I bring them in your grandfather wishes to see you." Peter's face reddened. "Umm…*immediately*, he stated. He didn't sound happy."

"Perfect," Quinn whispered to himself before eyeing his brother. "I'm sure he's been fit to be tied?"

"He was ready to send out the Red Guard looking for you. I told him to let you have the time to yourself. You needed it."

"Thanks," Quinn murmured, smiling at his brother. Thankfully, someone was on his side. "I appreciate it."

"No problem," Beau said before rising. "Want me to go with? As backup?"

"No, I think I need to handle this alone." He didn't need a witness to the dressing down he was likely to be on the receiving end of. But before he left, he turned back to Beau. "Charles?"

Beau's face went bright red. "He argued. Flat-out refused to leave. I tried to get tough… and that's when he put his hands down my pants."

Quinn rolled his eyes. Sex was a weapon for the beta. Charles knew how to use it well. He hadn't expected the man to turn it on Beau, though. Not when he was begging to stay with Quinn.

"When he knelt and insisted he was going to blow me, I left. I know I promised to get him out, but that guy's like wrestling an oiled snake."

"Sorry I put you in that situation," Quinn said. "I think I finally managed to get him out."

"Is he gonna stay out?" Beau asked, lifting a brow.

How the hell do I know? He waved at his brother and headed to the elevator. Once Quinn entered his grandfather's office, he sensed tension in the room. He was sure his grandfather wasn't happy about his sudden absence or the lack of information surrounding it—or could it be more to the old man's rancor? "Grandfather? You wished to see me?"

Tolliver lifted his stare from something he was reading and eyed him. There was no welcoming smile. The man's lips set in a firm line. Quinn had seen the look before, usually when his grandfather was facing an adversary across a boardroom table. Never once had he seen it turned on him. "You had us worried. No communication. You fell off the map and waltz back in here like nothing happened?"

"I wouldn't call it waltzing."

"I am in no mood for humor this morning, boy."

"I asked Beau to let you know I was leaving town for a few days."

"He did. But then a few days stretched on into the workweek and we'd still heard nothing from you. They had no phones where you were? You couldn't have checked in?"

"I was... *indisposed*."

Tolliver glared at him, but the anger soon faded. "So I hear you and Charles are no more."

"Correct," Quinn murmured before taking a seat across from the old man.

"Why?"

"I found him in my bed with Hagar," Quinn said bluntly, assuming his brother had likely neglected to share that particular news.

Tolliver waved his hand before him, as if the news was too trivial for him to hear. "You're ending a beneficial relationship over a mistake. Have you not made a mistake before, son?"

Quinn didn't like how much his grandfather sounded like Charles. "I doubt it was *one* mistake. It was just the *one time* he was caught," Quinn said before steeling himself. He wouldn't have his grandfather meddling in his relationships any further. "And to be honest, I shouldn't have to sit here and discuss my private life with you. What happens when I'm away from this building is none of your concern."

"You're wrong about that," Tolliver snarled. "One day, you will lead this company in my stead and I need to know you have the solid foundation under your feet that you need."

"A cheating beta who can't give me children is a solid foundation? I think not."

"Charles is the kind of husband you need. One who understands wealth and power. One raised in a family much like your own. You're different than others, you and Charles. He will lift you up... he will be the perfect mate. There at your side when you need him without putting demands on you. You'd still be free to find an omega. More than one, if you so choose. You'd have the money to set them up in apartments… where you can sate your lusts in private. Like the one you were with this weekend."

Quinn eyed his grandfather, stunned.

"You think I didn't have someone check in on you when you didn't answer calls?" Tolliver asked. "You are my heir, are you not?"

Quinn didn't answer.

"What is he to you? This omega."

Quinn knew what the true question was. "He's not my bond-mate, if that's what you're asking."

"Thank heavens," Tolliver murmured under his breath before pausing, playing with a file on his desk. He lifted his stare, a smile to his eyes but not his lips. "Did you use protection? I surely hope you did."

Quinn's face flamed. "I won't discuss this with you."

Tolliver's stare roamed over him, sizing him up, it seemed. "No matter. If he's pregnant, you'll have the child you need." The old man paused, looking at something on his desk. "Tanner's little friend is handsome. He could likely give you *many* children. Children you could raise with Charles."

"No," Quinn said. "I won't be raising any children with Charles."

Tolliver scoffed. "Whyever not?"

"The omega deserves better than that."

His grandfather frowned. "Deserves better? As in, he deserves… *you*?"

Quinn scowled. "I barely know him." *But I want to know more.* "And even if the laws state that we can mate who we choose, it doesn't mean he'd be willing to accept an alpha who wasn't his bond-mate."

"Oh, come now, boy. You don't think this omega would let go of his golden goose, do you?"

"Are you trying to say Bellamy set all this up? As if he would know that I would find Charles in bed with my cousin, and happen to get the keys to the lake house on *just* that weekend… where he could seduce me and get himself knocked up?"

"I didn't say that. But he's likely an enterprising young omega who knows what happened into his lap."

"He's not like that." In all honesty, Quinn didn't know that, but he sensed it soul deep. The omega had fought him, arguing at every turn. That wasn't the behavior of a man seeking to latch on to a rich alpha.

"Are you really imagining your life with this virtual stranger? You have no idea who he is."

"Like I said. What I do outside this building is none of your concern." Quinn lifted his chin, rising. "I'm done with this conversation."

"You need a mate at your side that can help you in society. Charles is that man. Not this… oh what was he?" Tolliver flipped open a file and scanned the page a moment. "*Interior designer?* A servant to the wealthy. That's all he is. Likely looking for a way to pull himself upwards. You're his golden ticket, my boy."

Rage swept through Quinn. *"You had him investigated?"*

"Of course I did! What you did was foolish and could've potentially destroyed you and this company, boy. You don't know who he is. What he's capable of. He trapped you in that house, and I bet he'll come running back in a month, claiming he's pregnant.

He'll expect you to mate him… and the only way to prevent that is to already be bound to Charles."

An image of Bellamy round and full with his child crossed his mind, and not for the first time.

"Charles and I *aren't* a good match… I want…" He paused, his mind trapped once again in the weekend in bed with Bellamy. "Passion. I want passion, and I get nothing from Charles."

"Passion can bring a man like us to our knees. It almost destroyed me, Quinn. Save yourself from that. Passion? Love? They create weaknesses. Marriage should simply be a business opportunity—one where you build bridges and amass more power. Charles will give you that in spades."

"You cannot force me into mating a man I don't want," Quinn said.

"I'm not trying to force you into anything more than seeing reason. Mating Charles will amass a family fortune unlike most people will ever see. You would ensure this family remains powerful for generations to come."

"By sacrificing what I want." He didn't even know what he wanted… yet he'd be sealing his fate by mating Charles.

"Family *is* sacrifice," Tolliver said. "I've sacrificed all for this family. For you. And your brothers."

Quinn shook his head, disturbed. "Just what did you sacrifice?"

Tolliver went silent. He didn't respond, and Quinn feared he didn't want to know the answer.

"Just consider what Charles can bring to you and to this family," Tolliver finally said. "You could have *everything*, boy. A powerful mate at your side. Wealth beyond your dreams. The omega you want tucked away. Children. *A legacy*."

Quinn shook his head. "I know you're accustomed to being able to control people… but this time, Grandfather, I won't dance to your tune." He eyed the old man. "I've given you everything I've got. I work myself to the bone. That's the sacrifice I'm willing to give. Not my happiness."

"Love is pain."

Quinn wished he knew more about his grandfather's past. Tolliver remained mum on most topics, the emotion of them apparently too much to endure. "In all things, you've told me to never give up. To push through the pain. To push through rejection. To reach for what I wanted." He paused, staring at his grandfather. "Yet because *you* were hurt along the way, you want me to give up on my chance at happiness… because if you couldn't make things work in your life, apparently no one can."

"Tread carefully, boy."

"I *have* tread carefully. My whole life. I've done everything you wanted of me… I've learned the ins and outs of this business. Done things your way. I've played the dutiful grandson. But I put my foot down here and now."

"One week and this omega already has you changed."

"For the better, it seems," Quinn spat. "Maybe it did open my eyes to the potential I could have with my own bond-mate. A life outside these walls. If what I experienced with Bellamy is only half what I'll feel for my own omega, then I have an idea what I'd be passing up. Charles can't be that for me. He never will."

"And this omega. Bellamy Carter... what do you do about him? He could very well be pregnant with your child. A bond-mate could refuse you for less."

"I don't know what happens next. All I do know is I *will* have the freedom to make my own choices. My own mistakes. If I fail, I do it on my own terms, no matter what you think."

His grandfather stared at him, anger simmering in his eyes. "Fine. You want to make your own mistakes, then you go right ahead and do so. Not marrying Charles is a mistake, but you'll have to live with that regret one day. Not me."

"Exactly," Quinn said. "My regrets will be my own. Not yours."

Tolliver McCreary sat back in his chair, the leather creaking around him. A cold smile spread over his lips, and Quinn felt a tremor race down his spine.

"Live your life, boy. As you see fit."

****

A week later...

Tanner McCreary entered his family's business, sailing past security with a wave and a smile. In one hand, he carried a burlap-covered canvas, excited to show the unexpecting recipient. He knew the people moving through the lobby were staring at him as he coasted along—what, with his paint-splattered overalls, bright purple and blue hair, and devil-may-care attitude—but as advertised, he *didn't* care. Let them look. His last name was smacked on the side of the place, so he could do as he damned well pleased.

He slipped into one of the many elevators heading up, reveling in the worried looks from the other riders in the car. They were likely concerned some of the paint covering him would end up on their expensive suits and shoes. Just for laughs, he would sway close to this one and that, watching them cringe away from the corners of his eyes. *What destruction I could cause.*

By the time he reached a few floors below his destination, he found himself alone and out of people to toy with. *Snoooze.*

The doors opened on the top floor and he exited, a heat-seeking missile, searching for his target. Luckily, he found Quinn exactly where he expected. Sans assistant to stop his forward momentum.

"Hello, brother," he announced as he barged in.

Quinn lifted his head from whatever he was reading at his desk. A frown twisted his face into an angry mask. "What are you doing here?"

"Is that *any way* to welcome someone bearing gifts?" Tanner lifted the burlap-covered frame and wiggled it in the air. "I brought you something for your office."

"I don't have time for games. If there's something you need, just let my assistant know and I'll take care of it."

Tanner scowled. "Is that all I am to you now? A business transaction? You throw money my way in hopes I'll leave you alone."

Quinn sighed and sat back in his chair. He tossed the pen in his hand to the surface. "That's usually the only reason I see you. When you need money."

Tanner scoffed. "You've made it abundantly clear that my lifestyle bothers you, so I stopped coming to see you unless I needed you."

"Your lifestyle doesn't… bother me."

Tanner lifted a brow, knowing Quinn was full of shit.

"Okay… yes… are there more productive things you could be doing with your life? Absolutely. But this is your choice." Quinn got a weird look on his face. "If this makes you happy… then I have no right to try and make you stop."

Tanner eyed his brother, shocked with that response. "It does make me happy. Art is my life. I don't know who I'd be without it."

Quinn held his stare a moment, silent. "So, I hear I have a gift? Hopefully something I'll like." He rose from his desk as Tanner set the frame up on the small coffee table across from Quinn's desk.

The minute Quinn stood shoulder to shoulder with him, he explained a little before the unveiling. "I was inspired and I've been painting until the wee hours all through. I've only had about five hours of sleep in the last couple of days and this thing is still a tiny bit wet, but I had to come down here and show you." He pulled off the burlap and turned to look at Quinn, gauging his brother's reaction.

Quinn stood frozen, his eyes wide and his lips parted. Tanner could see the visceral reaction, and knew there was definitely something there.

His brother's skin reddened. Quinn licked his lips.

He turned to look at Tanner.

"You should've called me and told me he was going to be there. I never would've gone if I knew he was there."

Bullseye. Quinn's still got the hots for Bellamy. "I *did!* Yeah, sure, it was a bit late. My bad. But no one *ever* goes up there anymore. How was I supposed to know your relationship with Chuck imploded? You can't be mad at me because you ignore my calls and don't listen to my messages."

"*Charles.*"

"Whatever," Tanner said, rolling his eyes.

"You know full well what his name is. You went to school with him," Quinn said.

"And do you know what we called him then? UpChuck. Fitting, isn't it? He makes everyone want to vomit."

"I won't play schoolyard games, Tanner."

"No games… it just shows a long history of him being an asshole. He wasn't worth my time then, and he's not now, either," Tanner spat. "Had you listened to me when you started seeing that vile sack of skin, maybe you wouldn't be in the situation you are now." Tanner smiled. "But something tells me you rather liked being in the situation you are now." He paused. "Well, not *now*. I mean a few days ago. When you had my friend writhing under you." Tanner paused again, smiling. "Or are you one of those who likes to lay back and let the omega do all the work? Did he ride you like a bucking bronco, brother?"

"Enough," Quinn warned.

"Was it enough? Or are you already thinking about getting him under you again?" Tanner asked, pumping his hips for added effect.

"My gods, Tanner. Will you stop?"

"Never!"

"*This* is why I avoid your calls!"

Tanner grinned. "I like causing chaos in your tedious life. Without me, things would be stale. Grandfather-level stale."

"Our grandfather isn't stale."

"True. He's past stale and on to moldering." Tanner eyed his brother. "It's my job in life to counterbalance that man and ensure you don't turn out exactly like him."

Quinn stared at Tanner, a hint of a smile on his lips.

"Oh my gods… is that a smile?"

Quinn looked away… back at the painting. He grew quiet, appearing to soak it in.

"You think it looks like him?" Tanner asked, eyeing the portrait he'd done of Bellamy from memory.

Quinn took a step closer, his neck working hard to swallow. "It looks *exactly* like him."

"I kinda had a feeling you might like to have this," Tanner murmured, watching as emotions filled his brother's face. "A memento, of sorts."

Quinn's stare came to Tanner's for a second before the painting captured him again.

"Do you like it?" Tanner asked.

Quinn's lips stretched almost into a smile again, but before he allowed himself to show the emotion, a frown came in to destroy it. "He said he wanted us to forget what happened. Pretend it never did. *His* words. Not mine. I have to respect his wishes."

"Bellamy and I had a quick little conversation before I left the studio today. He gave me the deets I begged for, but I know he held back. He says you and he… you two aren't… you know… bondies. But something tells me he might've been lying."

Quinn's head whipped. He faced Tanner, his eyes large and round. "Lying?"

Tanner shrugged. "He got this weird look on his face when he was talking about you. Maybe he doesn't even realize he's lying… because he's lying to himself." Tanner shrugged again. "I could be wrong, of course. But I definitely got the vibe that there was more to the story." Quinn didn't say anything but Tanner could see that information was being processed. "And… then there's your reaction to the painting."

"What reaction?"

"Like you want to reach into it and pull Bellamy out. Bend him over the desk and do more wicked things to him."

Quinn stared, dumbfounded. "There was *no* reaction."

Oh yes there was. "Well, I need to take this back to the studio."

"I thought this was mine?"

"One—it's unfinished. I need to add some last-minute touches and get it framed. Two—you just said you couldn't take it, so I suppose it's still mine."

"I want it," Quinn growled.

"No reaction, hmm?" Tanner grinned when his brother's face reddened. "It should be ready by tomorrow lunchtime. You remember where my studio is, right?"

"I own the building," Quinn spat.

"Oh, I know. I just wanted to remind you my studio is just above Bellamy's office."

Quinn glared at him before shaking his head, another smile almost showing on his lips.

Tanner lowered the burlap and lifted the canvas in one hand. "I'll see you tomorrow. K-later-thanks-bye!"

Tanner marched out of Quinn's office, a broad smile on his lips. *He does not deserve me.*

One day he'll realize that.

Chapter Seven

Early the following morning…

Bellamy nearly tripped over the discarded duffel he'd dropped at the foot of the stairs and neglected since. He'd been so behind with work, he'd focused all his energies on that. That focus had helped him ignore the memories of five days of chaos at the lake house. Now that he'd nearly caught up on everything, he realized everything at home had fallen through the cracks. He lifted the duffel and carried it through the house to the laundry room. After starting a load, he unzipped the bag and began tossing items into the wash.

Until he came upon a sock that wasn't his.

Lifting it to his nose, he inhaled a little, knowing he was being stupid. But it was apparent the sock belonged to Quinn. Bellamy felt a spark of lust low in his belly and had to slam the sock down on the corner of the machine, releasing it like it was on fire. He continued to peek at it as he emptied the rest of the contents from his bag.

He carried it into the kitchen with him and abandoned it on the counter while he poured himself his morning cup of coffee. Bellamy sat on the stool, sipping from his cup, eyeing the sock, and wondering if returning it to its owner would be completely transparent or not.

I could see how I react… determine if he is my alpha…

But he won't know. Not until the scent blocker wears off. Until then, it would just be me, tormenting myself. *Maybe I should wait.*

Fortunately, the scent blockers worked both ways. It completely masked the alpha's ability to scent his omega… and it limited the power of the alpha's scent on the omega. An omega knew his mate… but could fight the powerful lust that typically happened on first meeting. In other words, his Scentex would prevent him from losing his mind and throwing himself at Quinn. Only once it was out of his system would they once again be enslaved to their lusts—heat or no heat.

Bellamy lifted his phone and scrolled a finger over the screen. He opened up his calendar. It was two and a half months before he was to take his next dose of the scent blocker—the shot lasted three months and he'd just had one before his heat—and then it might take a week or two before it would fade enough for Quinn to scent him.

If he didn't take it again.

Big if.

He was at the cusp of a new business venture. Bowing to his alpha could put an end to that. Bellamy didn't know Quinn well enough to know his views on omega rights. It hadn't come up while the man had been over him, thrusting deep.

Just the thought of that sent tendrils of lust coursing down Bellamy's spine.

He wanted Quinn again. And soon.

I need to stop this!

Again he eyed the sock, wondering if it was a mistake to pursue it. He shoved it into his satchel before heading out the door for another day at work. After he arrived, he couldn't stop thinking of the stupid piece of knitted material inside his bag. Hours later, when he realized there was no productivity until he returned it, he grabbed his bag. He turned the 'Out to Lunch' sign in the window and locked up before rushing to catch the cross-province bus.

A tremor raced up his spine as he took his seat.

He was about to see Quinn again. Would the alpha be excited to see him?

Of course not. He has no idea who he might be to me.

The rest of the ride was spent with his inner pendulum swaying between excitement and absolute dread—enough to make him almost feel seasick. He got off on the stop near McCreary Towers and lifted his stare to take in the enormity of the building. It was likely the tallest tower in the Province, as far as he could tell, and spoke to the wealth the family had.

I am so out of my league.

Before he lost his nerve, he entered the building and headed for the welcome desk.

A young beta smiled up at him. "Can I help you, sir?"

"I have… a… delivery… for Mr. Quinn McCreary."

"You can leave it here," the man said.

"I *must* deliver it to him directly. Those were my orders," he fibbed.

"The best you can likely do is get it into his assistant's hands," the man said, spinning a sign-in book around. "Sign on the dotted line."

Bellamy signed and was handed a pass.

"Floor seventy-five. Turn to your left when you exit the elevator."

"Thank you," Bellamy said, pinning the guest pass to his shirt. He followed the man's directions and came up to an empty desk where he assumed the assistant sat. The door behind it had a small golden plaque that read, *Quinn McCreary, Chief Executive Officer.*

Bellamy steeled himself, reaching into the bag and squeezing the sock. *He's going to see right through me.*

I should leave.

No… It's now or never.

He strode up to the double doors and knocked. They soon opened—and a blond man stood behind the doors. "Can I help you?"

This must be the assistant. "I was looking for Quinn McCreary."

An odd look crossed the man's face as he eyed Bellamy. "Oh, *do* come in."

Bellamy entered and saw no one else was in the office. The door clicked closed behind him, and he spun to see the blond man standing with his back to the entrance.

"You have some nerve coming here."

Bellamy frowned. "Do I know you?"

The beta glared. "Charles Macklin. Quinn's *fiancé.*"

Fiancé? A sick feeling churned in Bellamy's gut.

"I know all about you trapping him in the lake house and abusing him for your own needs. How dare you come here now? Haven't you hurt us enough?"

Not once had Quinn mentioned he was engaged, but then things had happened so quickly… and there hadn't been all that much talking in between. "I don't mean to be rude—but he's engaged to a… beta?"

Charles' eyes narrowed. "Thanks to your omega rights advocates, it's now legal for us to mate whomever we wish."

Inwardly, Bellamy was rolling his eyes. Of course a beta would use omega rights like a weapon. *Asshole.* "But… no offense… you can't give him children."

"No. I can't. But what I can give him is much better. I grew up in his world. I come from a wealthy, powerful family, just like Quinn. I understand him and how he thinks. I know what he wants in his future and what he's working so hard to attain. I'll be there to make sure he achieves his goals and becomes the paragon we all know he will."

"All well and good, but alphas and betas are a rare mix," Bellamy snapped, shocked the harsh words flew from his lips so easily. "That whole children thing can be a major hurdle."

"That's what surrogates are for. And who knows? Maybe you're pregnant with our first child right now. A child he and I can raise together."

Bellamy gasped. "I don't think so."

Charles smiled, a predatory look that Bellamy was quite sure looked better on a shark. "Do you really think the courts would allow the child to remain with an unmated omega versus a happily mated alpha? Especially one as rich as Quinn?"

Panic hit Bellamy in the gut. "I suppose we'll find out if it goes that far."

"Do you have the means to raise a child on your own? I mean, you have recently started your own business, correct? Building that business will take a lot of time and energy. And a lot of capital. Capital that Quinn and I could assist you with."

"By handing over my child? I think not." He shook his head… realizing how insane the conversation was. "I don't even know that I'm pregnant. So the suggestions you're making are a bit far flung at this point."

Charles reached into his pocket and fished out a card. He shoved it Bellamy's direction. "When you find out, you should call me. I'm sure we can come to amicable terms. Allow for your continued independence and help finance your dreams."

Bellamy glared at the man. "You can shove that card straight up your ass."

Charles' smile only widened. "Once he and I are mated, I've told Quinn he can keep you as his whore. As long as you don't make trouble for us, that is. What you're doing now is trouble... don't turn this into a negative situation. We could allow you to see the child on occasion, too. If you remembered your place."

"Fuck. You." Bellamy stalked out, anger fueling every step. By the time he got to the elevator bank, he slammed the button, wishing it was Charles' face instead.

Sell my child? What the fuck? This guy's a psycho!

The elevator pinged, and he slipped inside. Once the doors closed, he released a little breath, glad to have thick steel between him and the beta. Hot tears stung behind his eyes as the realization of that insane conversation began to sink in.

Quinn's engaged.

Mating a monster.

Who wants to buy my child, if I'm pregnant.

This day just turned into a nightmare. He reached into the bag and pulled out the sock that had been the catalyst for the whole mess and dropped it like it was on fire. Then he heard his phone ringing and fished his cell from his pocket.

One Wild Heat

Unknown Number. Great.

"Hello?" he spat angrily.

"Wow… you don't sound like you're having a good day," Quinn McCreary said from the opposite end.

****

While Bellamy was at McCreary Towers…

Quinn exited his parked car and eyed the small office under Tanner's art studio. When he'd bought the building, the glass had been soaped over in the two small offices on the first floor. He'd barely given them the once over with the realtor, as Tanner had said he'd likely use them as storage. The larger upstairs space had been what his youngest brother had clamored for.

The 'Gone to Lunch' sign hung above the handle, and he felt the disappointment hit. *Hard.* He strolled up to the glass and eyed the mess inside. Bolts of fabric were strewn everywhere. Furniture wrapped in plastic with tags taped on them were all clustered in one corner. A large desk laden with drawings, invoices, what looked to be pistachio shells, and markers was situated in the other corner. It was obvious that the space was too small for his needs, but Bellamy was just starting out, so maybe it was all he could afford.

I wonder how much Tanner is charging rent for the office?

Turning his head, he saw a small box labeled 'Take One.' He snaked his hand inside and pulled out a business card. It had Bellamy's smiling face on it, and that alone was enough to quicken his pulse.

And then he noticed the phone number. Quinn smiled.

Without another thought, he grabbed his cell and dialed the number. Maybe the omega wasn't far and they could share a lunch before he headed back to the office.

The call was picked up on the third ring. "Hello," Bellamy answered angrily.

"Wow… you don't sound like you're having a good day."

Silence fell on the other side.

"It's Quinn Mc—"

"I know who it is."

Quinn paused, sensing his timing was likely off. Or maybe it was the fact he wasn't abiding by their agreement to go back to being strangers. "I know you said we should forget one another… but I stopped by Tanner's studio and saw your office. Thought I'd just say hello. Maybe… I don't know… take you to lunch."

"Lunch?"

"Yeah… you gotta eat, right? If you're not too far away and haven't eaten yet, why don't we?"

"Maybe you should ask your fiancé to lunch."
Click.

Quinn moved the phone, staring at it a moment. *Fiancé?* Quickly redialing, he got Bellamy's voicemail.

"Look, I don't know what information you have, but it's wrong. I don't have a fiancé. I'm bound to no one. And I want to see you again. Call me. Please."

Maybe Tanner has some info for me. He climbed the stairs to Tanner's studio, but soon realized no one was there. "Tanner?"

After calling out a few more times and not getting an answer, he called his little brother. "Where are you?"

"Oh shit! I forgot you!" Tanner paused. "Sorry. But to be totally honest, I'm actually surprised you showed up. You must really like this omega to leave *work*."

Quinn sighed. "I don't know him, Tan."

"You know, I've asked you to come to my studio numerous times and you've never shown up. But you show up for B. I see how I rate."

"The last time I came when you called, I walked in on five naked omegas, covered in wet paint and writhing around on the floor in some choreographed insanity."

"That was an *amazing* installation and you know it. I had a write up in the newspaper after that showing. It put me on the local artist map."

"Amazing? Maybe. Art? I don't know."

"You're *so* boring," Tanner said. "You wouldn't see art if it came up and slapped you in the face." His brother paused. "Wow… that's actually an interesting idea. Art coming up and slapping you in the face… with a handful of paint. Oh… I *love* it."

Quinn pinched the bridge of his nose. "Tanner… focus. How far away are you? Can I get the painting or not?"

"I'm getting some framing nails—I was out. Then I need to stop by the artist supply and pick up some new paints and a few new brushes. And then there's this new vegan place that opened up on Broadmore that I really want to try."

"You're a vegan now?"

"I'm *half* vegan. Every other day."

"I don't think that's quite how it works, Tanner."

"You do you, bro, and I'll do me."

"On that note, I need to head back to the office. It sounds like your afternoon is full."

Tanner chuckled. "It is. I'll bring the painting to your house later tonight. Or tomorrow. Or maybe this weekend… depends on the muse."

"I look forward to it," Quinn murmured, knowing full well he'd likely never see that painting again.

If I have to show up every day to get it, I will.

It'll give me a chance to see Bellamy every day, too.

Fortunately, the drive back downtown was quicker than the drive out, and he made it back to the office in record time. After parking in the underground garage, he slipped into an elevator, kicking a small piece of fabric as he got in. He leaned over and saw a sock that looked like one he owned.

Odd. He lifted the material and tossed into the small wastebasket just outside his office. Peter wasn't at his desk, and his office door was ajar. As soon as he entered, someone was there waiting on him. *Charles.*

"Now is *not* a good time," Quinn blasted, pointing toward the door. "Get out."

Charles stalked closer, moving his hips in a sensual way. He laid his hand on Quinn's chest, smiling. "Come now, alpha. I know you're angry. I spoke to your grandfather—"

"You spoke to my grandfather?"

"Yes. He and I had a lovely conversation. Now I know the issue. You feel pressured into the idea of mating. I know how strong-willed you can be and you feel boxed in. I get it. But you have to see what you get from a merger of our two families… money… power… standing in the community… and me…"

A merger of two families… how disgusting a thought. Quinn stared down at the smiling beta, bile rising in his throat.

Another face replaced Charles'.

Bellamy…

At the thought of Bellamy leaning against his body, he tensed. He felt his shaft thicken and grow semi-hard. Sadly, Charles likely thought the reaction was for him.

"See? Your body remembers what it feels like to be inside me. You *want* me, Quinn. You know I've always made you feel good. We're excellent together. There's fire there, in our bed."

"A bed you sullied with another man."

Suddenly, there were tears in Charles' eyes. Fake tears, of course, brought on in an instant. "A mistake, Quinn. I was lonely. You work… *so* much…" Charles paused to dab at the corner of his eye. "Hagar is *so* very much like you… he looks a little like you… and that's what attracted me to him. It was like I was having you in my bed. That's what I wanted. You."

"Out," Quinn repeated, lifting his stare. The thought that his lazy, leech of a cousin was anything like him was agonizing.

"You're growing hard against me and you think I can't feel you stirring?" Charles looked over one shoulder before whipping his head back. He lowered one hand and caressed the hardening outline of Quinn's cock. "Why not throw me over that desk and remind yourself how good we are together? Drive that big dick of yours deep inside me and remind me who my master is."

"That hole of yours has known many masters, from what I hear."

Charles' eyes flashed in anger, but faded just as quickly. Again he caressed the outline of Quinn's cock. "Experience you have enjoyed time and time again. I don't recall getting any complaints after you've fucked that hole. And well. It's yours now. Completely. I swear it."

Quinn grabbed Charles' shoulders and pushed the man back a few paces. "*Enough.* You need to leave."

Panic filled Charles' eyes. "You *want* me."

"I don't. Trust me. This hard-on *isn't* for you."

Charles' face twisted in a mask of anger. "Is it for your little whore?"

Quinn was silent a moment as he struggled to keep up with Charles' changing tides of emotion. "Whore?"

"You think I don't know where you went? And who you were with?"

Quinn clenched his teeth a moment. "You have some gall considering the last time I saw you was *under my cousin.*" And then everything fell into place suddenly. "You talked to him, didn't you? Bellamy?"

"And if I did?"

"You told him we were engaged, didn't you?"

Charles smiled wickedly. "That omega can't give you what I can."

"Oh? You can give me children? Passion? Heat?" Memories of his weekend with Bellamy flooded his mind again and made his body ache for more. He fought back a moan of lust. Sadly, it was the wrong moment for him to feel the emotions racing through him. Forcing them back, he stared out the window, down at the city below.

"I can give you better things. Standing. Power. Wealth."

"I already *have* those things," Quinn murmured.

"Together, we will be unstoppable. A society husband, one who can throw the right parties. Help you network with the right people. Build your company into the most powerful entity in this province."

"There's more to life than money and the trappings they procure."

Charles paused, the anger fading until the beta's face was the blank mask Quinn was more accustomed to seeing. "How long has this affair with the omega been going on?"

Quinn waffled between the truth and a lie. "It's truly none of your business."

"I believe it is… because if you tossed me from your life for doing the very thing you'd been doing yourself, then I'd call you a hypocrite. Did you plan this heat with the omega? You raced out so quickly without giving me a chance… because you were going to him, weren't you?"

He wasn't going to tell Charles he'd just met Bellamy. It didn't paint things in a good picture, either way. "Regardless, it doesn't matter. You and I… are over."

Charles smiled, the look sickening to Quinn. There was an evilness behind it that shone through. "I think… that you just met this omega. That he drew you in… coming to you in heat… begging you to fill him with your child."

"He did nothing of the sort." Quinn knew that some of that was true, but they'd both been victims of happenstance.

Hadn't they? Quinn shook his head, knowing full well there was no way Bellamy could've known he and Charles would split up the very weekend he was going to the lake house.

"You trust this omega? Who according to your grandfather, you don't even know. A man who needs a wealthy alpha to help him out of a tight spot."

Quinn narrowed his eyes. *A tight spot you're putting him in.* "I had a sneaking sensation you two were conspiring against me."

"Like me, Tolliver sees reason. He sees what we could be together. He sees you need a man like me beside you."

Quinn smiled suddenly. "How long have you been meeting with him behind my back?"

"Ever since I stole your phone," Charles smiled. "I knew he'd take a call from his favorite grandson."

"How did you hack into my phone?"

"Hack? The password was your papa's birthday." Charles rolled his eyes. "You're too sentimental." He reached into his pants and withdrew Quinn's phone. Or rather, what was left of it. The glass was shattered and the case cracked in several places. "I *accidentally* ran over it a few times. *Sorry.*"

"This is really how you try to win me back? Conspire with my grandfather? Openly admit to theft and destruction of my property? Lie to people about us being engaged? None of these things make me want to rekindle a relationship with you. Quite the opposite."

"As far as the stolen cellphone, time was not on my side. Your grandfather and I understand what's good for you, even as you actively fight it. I did what I had to do to get through to you. To make you see reason. To see just how far I'm willing to go to keep you in my life." The beta moved closer again, trying to press himself against Quinn. "We were meant to be, Quinn."

"No," Quinn replied, before putting distance between them. He stepped behind his desk, glaring at Charles. "As I told my grandfather, I won't be forced into mating a man I don't love." Quinn scoffed. "Hell, I don't even *like* you anymore. Not after seeing this side of you."

"Oh? I always get what I want, Quinn. You know that."

"Not this time."

Charles' face twisted into a harsh mask. "Challenge accepted."

Quinn shook his head, already tired of the games. It was starting to be abundantly clear that Charles might have issues far greater than he'd realized. "I didn't toss down a gauntlet. It's *over*. Just walk away before this gets any uglier."

Yet, it seemed that Charles was only just beginning. "Bellamy Carter, born of the Eastern Provinces. Before his first heat, he was sent on a trip to visit with family friends. Soon after his return, he would've likely entered the Omega Quadrants there, imprisoned behind thick walls, awaiting his alpha. Only, he never returned. He's technically living *illegally* in the Western Provinces, but as our liberal government tends to overlook runaway omegas from harsher provinces, he has managed to remain here for some time. Grease the right palm and he'd find himself deported back east in a heartbeat."

Quinn stiffened.

"Wouldn't that be a terrible thing? Him deported east, possibly pregnant with your child?"

Quinn felt like he'd been socked in the gut. He lifted his stare to Charles. "You wouldn't."

"To get what I want? Oh yes, I would."

He eyed the beta, sick to his stomach. "You can't actually think I would play the dutiful husband after this?"

"If you wish to save Bellamy, then you mate *me*. Set him up in an apartment where you can put our children on him, if that's what you wish. He can be our surrogate, but nothing more. You and I can raise the children you put on him as our own."

Rage flew into Quinn. "Everyone would know the children aren't really yours. They'd know I had an omega tucked away and that I was cuckolding you."

Charles blanched. "No one will know the details. For all they know, it could've happened in some sterile lab somewhere. Discretion over your extra-marital affairs will be in our pre-nup, you'd best believe it."

"What about *your* affairs? How many men have you already fucked in this town?"

Charles' face reddened. "Push me, alpha, and I'll make sure your omega is behind a wall by tomorrow."

Quinn stared at Charles, knowing he couldn't allow that to happen. He stuffed the rage he felt and spouted a bold-faced lie. "I'll consider your terms."

Charles stared at Quinn a moment, as if sizing him up. "Consider quickly. I won't wait forever."

The beta exited. Quinn remained frozen to the spot where he stood, his mind racing. He shot a hand through his hair, unsure what to do next.

Mating Charles wasn't an option, but if he didn't, Bellamy could suffer.

What if the omega is pregnant?

Something his grandfather had said about Bellamy came back to him. *He'll expect you to mate him… and the only way to prevent that is to already be bound to Charles.* A smile came to his face. It was good advice…

If I mated Bellamy… he'd be mine. He couldn't be shipped off to the eastern provinces. He'd avoid incarceration in one of those barbaric Omega Quads or whatever they call them. And I couldn't mate Charles if I was already mated.

Quinn froze. He'd avoid mating one man and end up mated to another. *How is that any better?*

Because it would be Bellamy.

Quinn's mind went back to what Tanner had told him. *He's lying. There was something in his eyes…*

There's something about that omega… maybe he's not my bond-mate, but I'd likely have better chances at happiness with Bellamy than I would with Charles.

He glanced at his phone and recalled being hung up on.

First, I have to get him to speak to me.

Quinn redialed Bellamy's phone.

Time to turn on the charm.

"Hello, you've reached the phone of Bellamy Carter…"

Chapter Eight

Later that evening…

Once he arrived home after dark, Bellamy kicked the door closed behind him. He dropped his satchel by the door and collapsed into the first chair he reached, ignoring the pile of mail sitting on the floor.

"This has been the shittiest day of my life."

He scrubbed both hands over his face and tried to shove the pain he felt over learning the truth down deep. Both starving and not hungry, he rested a few more minutes, weighing his options. He doubted there was much of anything in the fridge. He'd bought a couple of slices of pizza on his way home the night before, but neglected to grab anything on his way that night.

"The one thing that *is* in the fridge is wine."

That got him on his feet in a jiffy. He was pouring himself a nice glass of red when there was a knock on the door. He froze, wondering if it was Quinn. The alpha had been blowing up his phone all day and he'd nearly gone nuts. He'd ignored them all, so maybe the man had given up on the calls and tried a more direct route.

When he reached the door, he peeked through the side curtain and saw it was an entirely different alpha. He opened the door and saw Fitz standing outside, looking rather glum.

"I'm not really in the mood for guests tonight. Today has been utterly terri—"

Fitz lifted a bag as Bellamy had begun to speak and the scent of take-out noodles hit his nose. His favorite.

"I was harsh on you when you returned, and I'm sorry." He smiled wanly. "I know how empty your refrigerator normally is, so I took a shot in the dark. Thought it would make up for me being a shitty friend."

"Why do you have to be so good to me? I don't deserve it."

"You do," Fitz murmured, walking in as Bellamy pushed the screen open for him. "I like taking care of you, Bell."

Bellamy hated when anyone called him Bell. He only let Fitz get away with it. On occasion. And considering the rumbling of his stomach and the smell of those noodles, he wasn't arguing over it. "I'll get the chopsticks." He strode into the kitchen. "Want some wine? I just opened some red."

"Should you be drinking?"

A reminder he just might be pregnant added to his trying day. He spun to glare at the alpha. "One, I might not be pregnant. And two, *one* glass of wine isn't going to cause issues. *If* there's even a baby."

Fitz's stare went to his flat stomach for a moment before it lifted. "A beer would be better for me. If you have one."

Bellamy opened the fridge and peeked inside. Beer wasn't his thing, but he found a couple of bottles. "Looks like there are some leftovers from one of your last visits."

"Perfect," Fitz said from just behind him.

A big arm reached in and took the bottle from his hand. When he closed the door and turned, Fitz was still too close. He stared down at Bellamy, adoration in his eyes.

"Fitz."

The alpha took a couple of steps back. "I know… I know."

They sat at the island and passed the boxes of noodles back and forth, filling their bowls. Silence filled the air after, other than the sound of chopsticks and slurping.

"So," Fitz said once they were nearly done. "Shitty day, hmm? Wanna talk about it?"

"Not really," Bellamy said.

Awkward silence filled the space after. Bellamy knew Fitz wanted to know, but it would just lead to them arguing. He was sure of it. And that's the last thing he needed.

A knock came to the door, and Bellamy tensed, wondering if that was the reason for his shitty day right there. He didn't need a brawl in his house, so he quickly raced to the door and peeked outside.

All he saw was a huge bouquet of flowers.

Sighing inwardly, he opened the door. The pimply-faced delivery guy eyed him. "Bellamy Carter?"

"Yes."

"These are for you."

The huge vase was handed over, and he reached for his pockets, realizing he had zero cash on hand. That big arm of Fitz' reached beside him, handing the driver a few *renos*. Heat filled his face, knowing full well who they were likely from… and knowing Fitz would ask questions. He shut the door and walked the arrangement into the kitchen, setting it on the end of the island.

"Fancy flowers. From a fancy-pants alpha?"

"No idea," Bellamy murmured, reaching inside the blooms to grab the card.

Call me. Please. I need to talk to you.
-Q

Bellamy ripped up the card and tossed it into the trash before returning to his stool to finish his noodles. Fitz remained standing a few feet away, an expectant look on his face.

"Your noodles are getting cold."

"Why Quinn McCreary? Couldn't it be *anyone else* but someone from that family?"

Bellamy slurped up his last bite. "What is it you have against the McCrearys anyway? I know you don't like Tanner, but I didn't know the hatred extended to the whole family."

"I don't dislike Tanner."

"It sure looks like you do."

"Well… he *is* a bit arrogant. Self-absorbed. Shallow. Has a nasty habit of flinging himself on me whenever I'm in the same room."

"Yeah, you *definitely* love him to pieces," Bellamy said sarcastically before rolling his eyes.

Fitz finally sat down at the island. He eyed his bowl before pushing it away, half-eaten. "I don't know… I just get agitated as soon as Tanner comes into a room. As far as the rest of that clan—have you not noticed that you can't toss a stick and not have it land on something that family owns?"

"Well, there are a lot of them. It's not all owned by Tanner and his branch. From what he's told me, there are millions of cousins."

"They're a plague," Fitz said. "You didn't grow up here, so you don't know how it is to not be a McCreary. They're like a pack of rabid wolves. They protect their own, circling their wagons. Either you're one of them or you're not. They own *everything* and act like everyone else is below them."

"So Tanner and his brothers have never done anything wrong to you personally?"

"No. Not personally," Fitz murmured before taking a drink from his beer and looking dejected. "Unless you count losing you to one."

"I belong to no one. Neither of you." Bellamy lifted a brow and waited to see if Fitz would try and argue the point. "I am my own person."

"Yet. You belong to no one… *yet*." Fitz lowered the bottle to the island. "McCrearys are known for getting whatever they want. And if Quinn McCreary wants you, he'll eventually get you."

"You have so little faith in me." *What am I saying? The man's my alpha.*

An engaged alpha, though.

Fitz shook his head. "I do have faith in you… but I also know how this family operates. They always win. *Always*."

Maybe not this time.

Neither of us will win.

"You can't let him in, Bellamy. Nip this in the bud."

Bellamy eyed the alpha. "I didn't know you had the right to dictate what I do and don't do… that's news to me!"

"I'm not trying to argue with you, but you don't understand these guys."

"These pushy, arrogant alphas who expect an omega to do exactly what they command?" He lifted one brow and glared at Fitz.

"I just want to protect you." Fitz rose, sighing. "I should go before we end up arguing. Let you have some quiet time to relax after that bad day you won't tell me about."

He sensed Fitz was fishing, but he wasn't biting. Bellamy rode the line between anger and exhaustion and just didn't have the energy to continue tossing barbs back and forth, especially as he knew Fitz was only trying to help. Even if it wasn't helping at all. "Thanks for dinner." He walked Fitz to the door. "I appreciate it more than you know."

Fitz leaned in and Bellamy tensed, slightly pulling away. He immediately regretted backing away when he saw the hurt look on Fitz's face. The alpha eyed him before kissing his cheek. He opened the door. "Glad I could help a little. Night."

"Night."

Bellamy closed and locked the door before spinning to look at the huge vase full of flowers decorating his kitchen. He reached into his pocket and pulled out his cell phone, looking over the crazy number of voicemails awaiting him. After finding a comfortable spot on the couch, he began listening and kept hearing the same thing over and over again.

I'm not engaged.
It's all lies.
I want to see you.
Call me.

When he'd listened to the last one, he lowered the phone, not sure who to believe. After hearing the things Fitz had said about McCrearys getting whatever they wanted, he had to wonder. Was Quinn lying so he could get his way, or was he telling the truth?

Technically, Quinn owed him nothing—their days together had been an accidental happenstance and the man didn't know they were bond-mates. Bellamy had no right to feel angry over the fact Quinn might be engaged, even if he did in some small way. Would the alpha truly try to use subterfuge to get everything he wanted? A beta husband and a pregnant omega tucked away?

His gut told him Quinn was telling the truth, but something Charles had said played back over and over in his mind. *I've told him he can keep you as his whore. As long as you don't make trouble for us, that is.*

Those words made his blood run cold.

I won't be anyone's whore.

He was still too stunned from Charles' news… and utterly exhausted. In other words, he wasn't in the right mind to be talking to anyone, especially Quinn. He needed time to think and take a step back before he made himself an emotional fool over a man—even if fate said that man belonged to him. Bellamy tossed the phone to the side, still feeling the desire to dial that number.

Just to hear his voice.

Memories of the way the baritone had vibrated down his spine while he'd been in heat flashed into his mind. *My gods, I need to get him out of my head!*

A bubblebath. That *sounds wonderful.*

He cleaned up the kitchen a little before he headed upstairs to fill the tub—where he lost himself for a good hour before collapsing into bed.

Later, he drifted off to sleep.

Dreaming of Quinn.

****

The worst timing ever…

"Sir? Mr. Barrington is on line one," Quinn's assistant buzzed in with. "Says it's urgent."

"Thanks," he murmured before grabbing his phone and hitting the button. Barrington Industries had been his main focus… until Bellamy had come into the picture. What had he potentially let slip? "Soren, how are you?"

"Not good," Soren Barrington said on the other end. "We're hearing stories about your plans for our company… and it's not what was discussed in our meetings. The workers have heard and just walked off the job! We're in utter chaos here, with the labor unions screaming from one end and the media on the other. It's already hit the local news… and there's a chance it could go wider considering the buy-out."

Fuck. "What stories?"

"That you're planning to break us apart and sell off the company piecemeal. The workers are terrified. If they don't get back to work, and soon, we're going to lose several important contracts—which is a problem *you* will inherit."

"I don't know where this news is coming from," Quinn said, wincing. "We aren't breaking up the company… we made promises."

"Then you need to speak to your grandfather. The sources are saying it came straight from his lips."

Quinn sighed inwardly. The Barrington deal was his, not his grandfather's. He spent the next few minutes ironing out some details before realizing he'd have to travel to clear everything up prior to completing the sale. As soon as he had Soren calmed, he headed up to speak to his grandfather to find out where the misinformation had come from.

He found Tolliver sitting behind his huge desk, reading reports.

Upside-down reports.

Quinn frowned, a niggle of worry filling him. "I just got a call from Soren Barrington. The workers staged a walk-out over news we're selling the company off in pieces."

"That *is* what you plan, isn't it?" Tolliver said as he tossed the file to his desk.

"I emailed you before my trip, saying I was reconsidering that plan after talking to Beau. And even if that *was* the plan, leaking that news to the press *wasn't* a good idea. We've already signed the papers… if their stock tanks, we could lose our asses. Now I have to fly out there and clean up this mess to make sure we don't."

Tolliver scowled. "And this is my fault, how?"

Quinn paused, taking a deep breath. "The press says their source was you."

His grandfather got an odd look on his face—as if he was searching his memory. And then he suddenly became angry. "I didn't say anything to anyone. How dare you toss accusations my way! I built this company… why would I…" His grandfather frowned, hesitating mid-sentence. Silence filled in between them.

Quinn's frown grew. "Grandfather?"

Tolliver lifted his stare, looking confused. "Yes?"

It was then that he knew something was wrong. "You were saying you didn't tell anyone about our plans for Barrington Industries."

Tolliver scratched his head. "There was a man in the elevator a few days ago… asking questions." He lifted his stare, panic in his eyes. "Maybe I did."

Quinn saw the uncertainty in his grandfather's lost expression and couldn't feel angry any longer. "We need to get you in to see a doctor. I'll call Beau and have him take you as soon as possible... I've got to get a flight out today."

His grandfather remained silent before picking up a file from his desk and opening it. Quinn backed away, reaching for his phone. As soon as he was outside, he turned to Tolliver's assistant. "Have you noticed anything out of the ordinary with my grandfather?"

The assistant, Joshua, looked up at Quinn sheepishly. "Like what?"

"Memory issues?"

The older beta looked down.

"Joshua?" Quinn asked, his tone firm when the beta didn't reply.

"For a few months now. It started slowly... but the last couple of weeks... it's gotten worse."

"You should've told me," Quinn snapped angrily.

"He made me promise not to," Joshua said, a man who'd worked for his grandfather for a good thirty years. "I owed him a little time before he was kicked out of the company he founded. He *loves* this place."

Quinn sighed. "He does. And I wouldn't summarily kick him out, either. But we should've known... he needs medical care." He lifted his phone, readying to call his brother.

"He's *seen* a doctor."

Quinn whipped his head up. "He has?"

"It's dementia."

He stood there, hearing that word, and felt the air sucked out of his lungs. Dementia. Quinn didn't know much about the disease, but what little he did had him terrified. Everything his grandfather was would disappear. The money, the power, the prestige… it wouldn't save him in the end.

When he felt like the world had stopped spinning, he called Beau. He hated leaving in that moment, but he had to go stop the bleeding before it got any worse.

Chapter Nine

Five days later…

Bellamy heard the bell over his door and lifted his head… just in time to see yet *another* floral delivery to his office. He glanced around his already claustrophobic office littered with vases. Every single day, he got a delivery. Sometimes two. One at the office during the day… and possibly another in the evening at home. He'd tried to refuse them, but the drivers simply left them on the steps outside or the sidewalk. After he'd called the florist and demanded no more, Quinn just found another florist.

"Someone die?" the newest driver asked, glancing around.

"No, but if I get one more delivery, someone just might."

The young beta frowned, not seeming to understand. He shrugged, apparently past caring. "You Bellamy Carter?"

"Will it help if I say no?"

"You're *not* Bellamy Carter?" the man asked, clearly confused.

"Just give me the flowers," Bellamy said as he rose from his desk. He handed the delivery driver his last five reno and bid the man adieu. Once he found a bare spot to set the new vase, he eyed the card peeking out through the long-stemmed roses. He'd been ignoring the cards, hoping the endless parade of flowers would eventually stop, but Quinn had a tenacity Bellamy hadn't quite expected.

And he hated to admit that he liked the attention some. He should've put his foot down sooner… but at that point, it was starting to go overboard.

Way past overboard at this point.

This needs to stop.

He reached in for the small white envelope and opened it.

Almost home… I'll see you soon…

-Q

Almost home? What did that mean? Suddenly curious, Bellamy searched through the other cards, looking for clues. Finally, he found the one he needed.

Have to fly out for a few days on business… we WILL talk when I get back…

-Q

Bellamy sighed. All he had to do was call Quinn and he could end it. But he also feared he wouldn't be able to say no if he spoke to the alpha again. Turning back to his desk, he gazed through the plate glass window and saw Quinn stepping out of his red sportscar, parked just down the street.

Shit!

Bellamy wasn't ready for that conversation. Not yet. He ducked into the small backroom where he stored pieces of furniture and samples, hiding from sight. The bell on the door clanged, and he heard footsteps into the office.

"Hello?" Quinn paused before calling out again. "Bellamy?"

Quietly stepping over a few end tables he still needed to deliver, Bellamy hedged closer to the back door.

"Bellamy? I *know* I saw someone in here when I pulled up," Quinn said, his voice strong and clear.

And *clearly* doing things to Bellamy's libido. He felt a tremor of need move down his spine… as his cock thickened.

"Come on… let's talk, Bell."

Bellamy froze and glared toward the front of the office. He wanted to argue and tell Quinn to never call him that again, but bit his tongue. All while turning the knob on the back door. He wedged himself outside and slowly closed the door before racing up the back stairwell to Tanner's studio.

Tanner lifted his head from his work and narrowed his stare. "Who're you running from?"

"Your brother," Bellamy said before sneaking behind a few canvasses leaning against one wall.

"Why? What has Quinn done?"

Footsteps sounded on the stairs below, and Bellamy tensed. "Please," he whispered. "I'll tell you when he's gone."

Tanner nodded before turning with a brilliant smile for his brother. "Quinn, darling. What're you doing here?"

"I came for my painting. And I'd hoped to speak with Bellamy… but he's not downstairs."

"Maybe he had an appointment. He's in and out most days."

"With the doors unlocked and no sign on the door?" Quinn paused. "You don't think something's wrong, do you? I looked around, but I didn't see anything amiss." He paused again. "Maybe I should call the guard."

"No, no, no… he's fine," Tanner said. "He can be a little absent-minded and leaves his office unlocked at times. I'm sure he's okay. This neighborhood is pretty quiet. It's why I chose it."

"He should take better care of himself and his business," Quinn snapped.

"I'll pass along the message," Tanner murmured, glancing at Bellamy from the corner of his eye. "Which I'm sure he will take kindly. We omegas love having orders barked at us from alphas."

Bellamy had to put a hand over his mouth to cover his chuckle. What he wouldn't have done to see the look on Quinn's face after that, especially as he didn't *verbally* respond to Tanner's comment.

"Have you seen him today?" Quinn asked.

"Who?" Tanner asked with a grin.

"Bellamy," Quinn said, sounding irritated.

"Oh, yes. This morning as I came in. He was working away in his little floral paradise." Tanner grinned widely. "A bit much… but I might steal one or two to use as my muse. I haven't done a still life in *forever.*"

Bellamy heard Quinn's footsteps growing closer. He worried Quinn might be able to see him if the alpha moved too close.

"Tell him I stopped by… please. He won't answer my calls."

"What did you do to him?"

"None of your concern," Quinn muttered. "So… my painting? Where is it?"

"Maybe you're no longer worthy to have it," Tanner said, lifting his chin arrogantly.

Quinn sighed. "You said it was a gift."

"Gift, schmift," Tanner said, waving a hand. "If you can't treat my friend with respect, you don't deserve my gifts, big brother."

"I didn't disrespect him. He heard a lie and apparently doesn't believe the truth."

"*Your* truth. Truth is a very elastic thing. Point of view can warp it immensely. The way you see things and the way he sees things might be absolutely different," Tanner said, smirking. "Maybe you should tell me more so I can determine what is and isn't the truth."

"It's… none… of… your… business…" Quinn's voice seemed to be getting more distant as he walked away. "I'm calling you later… to make sure he's okay. I'm worried."

"K-later-thanks-byeeeee," Tanner called out before Bellamy heard Quinn's steps down the stairs and the door shut at the bottom.

He waited another few seconds, just to be sure Quinn was actually gone.

"So… what lie did he tell you?" Tanner asked, spinning on his stool to face Bellamy.

"He didn't. Someone named Charles informed me that he and Quinn are engaged."

Tanner let out a laugh. "No, they're not." The smile faded from his face. "He damned well better not be… I mean, unless it *just* happened… but I seriously doubt that. Last time I spoke to Quinn, he and Charles had just broken up."

Damn.

Why *hadn't* he just asked Tanner in the first place?

Bellamy flew down the stairs, just in time to see Quinn's red sports car pulling away. He tried to wave the man down, but it was useless. After going back into his office, he spied all the flowers filling the space. Maybe he hadn't given the alpha the chance the man deserved.

He reached into his pocket and grabbed his phone before dialing Quinn's number.

It picked up on the first ring.

"Are you safe?"

Bellamy sighed at the worried tone to Quinn's voice. "Yes."

"I just stopped by your office and it was open, with no one inside. I worried something had happened to you." Quinn paused. "Although I was quite sure I saw you in there as I pulled up."

Cringing, Bellamy crossed his fingers, not wanting to tell the man he'd out and out hid. "I was across the street, helping a neighbor for a moment. I didn't think to lock up, being so close," he fibbed. "Sorry if I made you worry."

"Make it up to me?"

Bellamy tried not to smile. "How?"

"Have dinner with me tonight."

Bellamy leaned up against his office window. "I suppose. Or how about you come to my house… and I cook you dinner?"

There was a bit of silence on the other end, and Bellamy wondered if that was an issue.

"Are you sure we should be alone?" Quinn finally asked. "I figured being out would put you more at ease."

Bellamy smiled, appreciating the alpha's consideration. "Can I trust you to not pounce on me?"

Quinn chuckled. "To be honest, I don't know if I trust myself around you. I can't stop thinking about you, Bell."

There it was again. *Bell.* But without the ire he'd felt moments ago. He actually liked the sound of it coming from Quinn's lips. Especially when it came with a seductive admission he could make himself, as well. *I can't stop thinking of you, either.* "I figured we have some… *stuff*… to talk about. Personal stuff. Being alone might be the right place for that."

"True." Quinn was silent a moment. "Can you cook?"

"Of course I can cook," Bellamy outright lied, knowing he was picking up take-out from the diner on the corner on the way home. "Do you have any requests?"

"Surprise me," Quinn murmured. "What time?"

"Say… seven?"

"It's a date," Quinn said before adding huskily, "We'll talk more tonight… I can't wait to see you."

Bellamy smiled. "Me either."

****

Just before seven…

Bellamy tossed the take-out boxes into the trash, sprinkled some shredded cheese over the lasagna he'd picked up, and slid both small casserole dishes into the oven to rewarm their dinner. Afterwards, he set a nice table, adding one of the many vases of flowers to the center, and stood back to admire the setting. A knock sounded a few minutes early.

He tried not to rush to the door. Pausing midway, he took a deep breath, trying to calm the butterflies in his belly. When he finally opened up…

It was Fitz leaning in the doorway. "Wanna grab a bite?"

"I can't… I've got plans."

"Where are you going?"

"Nowhere," Bellamy answered.

Fitz stood up straighter, both brows moving into a tight line. "You have a guest?"

"And if I do?"

Fitz's jaw tensed. "None of my business. Right?"

"Fitz…"

As the alpha turned to leave, who showed up but Quinn. In an instant, both of them were standing toe to toe, glaring as Bellamy slid outside and moved between them. He put his back to Fitz and eyed Quinn.

"My friend, Fitz, was just checking in on me. He's on his way out," Bellamy said to Quinn as he heard them both growl at one another.

Great. Two alphas in a pissing contest just outside my door. The rumbles raced through like fire in his veins. Biting his tongue, he bit back a moan rising to his lips. He hated drama… but the inner animal within was eating it up. Heat spread through him, ready to give in to the alpha who won the battle. A little slick eased from him, and suddenly, both alphas were looking down at him—lust in their eyes.

Fitz took a step back, glaring wearily at Bellamy. He seemed to struggle to lift his gaze to Quinn. "You hurt him, and you deal with me."

"Let me guess… you're the alpha I scented on him while he was moaning under me," Quinn replied menacingly.

Fitz rushed Quinn, nearly knocking Bellamy over. "Just like a McCreary… you feel the need to mark everything as yours."

"Stop!" Bellamy screamed. "Stop this right now!"

Quinn lifted his chin, and neither man backed off.

Bellamy glared at Quinn. "Or you can *both* leave!"

Quinn growled before taking a half-step back. "For you, I'll back off… for *you*. Not him."

"I don't need favors from you, McCreary," Fitz snapped.

"Go!" Bellamy cried at Fitz over his shoulder.

Fitz's face crumped in a look of pain. Finally, he walked away, and Bellamy worried he'd just destroyed that friendship. Bellamy knew alphas were territorial and didn't like to share their toys—but it was the first time he had two prime bulls fighting over him and it felt both disturbing and exhilarating at the same time. And now he better understood why some provinces felt the need to put their omegas behind walls. It wasn't so much to imprison them, but save them from stupid bullshit like that.

"Who is he to you?" Quinn all but growled.

Bellamy spun to face the alpha. "A friend."

"I recognize his scent… he's more than a friend to you. You. Are. Mine!"

"I'm not!" Yet Bellamy's body flooded with desire at those words. "I owe you *no* explanations… my life is my own. Before *and* after that wild heat. I belong to no alpha."

Quinn stood silently on the sidewalk, his chest heaving as he panted. After a moment, he lowered his head. "I'm sorry," Quinn mumbled beside him. "I don't know what got into me. I've never done that... *ever.*"

Bellamy turned to face him, inwardly gasping as another wave of need hit. "Don't let it happen again. *Control* yourself." The last bit was almost more for himself than the alpha.

Quinn held his stare. "I'll do my very best." He lifted his hands... where he held a bottle of sparkling grape juice and another damned bouquet of flowers.

"You brought me *more* flowers?"

Quinn chuckled. "I didn't want to arrive empty handed and... I wasn't sure how many of them ended up in the trash."

"I didn't throw any of them away, but you best be sure I'm looking into places to donate a few," Bellamy said before welcoming the alpha into his home.

"Donate them?"

"As if I need nearly two dozen arrangements," Bellamy said as he shut the door. "There are likely some seniors who would love to have their rooms brightened up with some lovely flowers."

"You've got a kind heart." Quinn chuckled. "I need to remember to call the florist in the morning. You might end up with a couple of more before I can cancel the orders."

Bellamy sighed, trying not to laugh. "You do realize that can be considered harassment, right?"

Quinn shrugged. "I'm not used to being ignored. I didn't know what else to do to get your attention without crossing the line into stalking."

Bellamy took the flowers and cold bottle from him before crossing into the kitchen. He wanted to shove the bottle down the front of his pants to cool him off and stop the burgeoning erection tenting his pants. *Thank the gods for kimonos to hide things like that.* "Can I get you something to drink?"

"Whatever you're having," Quinn murmured as the alpha leisurely inspected his living area.

Bellamy's townhouse was one of his projects, used to photograph for his portfolio. He'd put a lot of time and energy into the design. He absolutely loved the mixes of fabrics and colors. It was gorgeous… and homey, too.

"I assume you decorated?" Quinn asked, still searching over his belongings.

Bellamy noticed the man took quite an interest in the photos scattered about in frames. "I did. Do you like?"

"Not exactly my style, but I do like it," the alpha murmured, slowing walking closer to the kitchen. "It fits you."

"How so?" Bellamy asked, opening a bottle of sparkling water and pouring it over the glass of ice he'd made.

"Stylish yet still feels comfortable."

Bellamy couldn't hide the heating of his cheeks. He handed the glass of water to Quinn. "That was exactly what I was going for." Their fingers met as Quinn took the glass, and he nearly hissed in torment. He winced, trying to hold back the lust screaming within.

"Everything okay?"

You're mine. My bond-mate. You just don't know it yet. How unfair it was that only he had that knowledge…

but then, maybe it was a blessing, too. He still had questions. "I'm fine. Will be better once I know this truth of yours."

Quinn took a sip from his glass before laying it onto the island. "Charles and I dated for a few years. We lived together. It's over, and he's not willing to face that. He and my grandfather both think we should mate… which is hilarious because the reason both Charles and I began dating was to help potentially stop our families from setting us up with others and delay the whole mating idea."

"Why does your grandfather want you two to mate?"

Quinn sighed. "Simply put? He's loaded and his father is unwell. My grandfather sees a business opportunity. I do not." The alpha began to say something more, but hesitated.

"What?"

Quinn shook his head. "Nothing."

Bellamy felt the alpha was hiding something, but he decided to let it go… "Was I the cause for the end of this relationship?"

"No. I caught Charles in bed with one of my cousins. I'd broken things off just before I went up to the lake house. I was going there to get away from the drama and have some quiet…"

"And ended up getting snagged into an even bigger drama."

Quinn smiled. "It wasn't what I expected. I didn't get the message you were there, I swear. I wouldn't have put either of us in that situation… but I don't regret being there with you, either." The man paused, looking away a moment. "I know we're not bond-mates and you wanted to forget this happened."

He lifted his stare and met Bellamy's. "I can't forget you. Morning, noon, and night, all I think about is you. I know you said it was this wild heat, but we've been apart for weeks and I can't stop wanting to be with you."

"I can't stop thinking about you, either," Bellamy admitted.

Quinn moved around the island and drew Bellamy into his arms. The kiss that came was combustible. The alpha feasted on his lips, and Bellamy fought right back, warring with Quinn's tongue. Their hands searched over one another, searching for the soft spots... the places that would set them ablaze.

The alpha was skilled at finding all of Bellamy's. One by one, he found each and exploited them. Bellamy could barely remain standing. He trembled all over, his slick coating his ass.

"Quinn," he said and could hear the pleading need in his voice.

The alpha lifted him. This time, Bellamy didn't argue. He needed too much and wasn't sure his legs would work.

"Upstairs?" Quinn asked between seeking kisses.

"Yesss," Bellamy hissed.

The alpha marched them up the narrow stairs, somehow without teetering one bit. Bellamy struggled to do that alone and sober. Quinn seemed to home in on his room and he soon found himself deposited in the middle of his own bed. Clothes went flying until two naked bodies collided. Quinn took his time, licking and tasting every inch when all Bellamy wanted was to feel that big, thick, pulsing dick sliding home.

"Fuck me, my alpha," Bellamy pleaded, but he was denied.

Quinn's mouth trailed down his neck and to one pointed nipple. The alpha suckled on it, drawing it into his mouth before rolling it with his tongue. After, the second got the same treatment. Quinn then moved down Bellamy's stomach, pausing midway.

"I want to put a baby here," Quinn whispered. "If I haven't already."

Bellamy wasn't in heat, yet those words had almost as strong an impact on him as if he was. For the alpha to say it? It gave him pause. He had to force the next words from his lips. "I'm not ready for a baby. Not yet."

Luckily, he couldn't become pregnant outside his heat. They could play all they wanted without protection… until the next heat came around.

"What if I've already done it?" Quinn whispered. "My seed could already grow inside you."

Bellamy struggled to bite back the moan. "It might."

"You'll be beautiful… big and swollen with my child."

Bellamy's lids fluttered closed, the image coming to his own mind.

Quinn continued on down before engulfing the head of Bellamy's cock between his lips. After that, Bellamy lost conscious thought. Quinn's hot, wicked mouth brought him to the edge… only to have his release stolen from him.

Not once…

But twice.

"Quinn," he moaned, thrusting his hips up and trying to force the alpha to let him come.

"Not yet, sweetheart."

Bellamy thrust again, demanding satiation. *"I need…"*

"I know, baby," Quinn murmured, sliding two thick fingers into Bellamy's slickened ass. "I know *exactly* what you need."

The alpha pumped those fingers deep while he returned to suckling Bellamy's cock. Quinn hollowed his cheeks, sucking every inch… from base to tip. Bellamy could feel him leaking—both slick from his ass and pre-cum from his cock. His body was primed and ready… only he needed the alpha to give him more.

"Quinn!"

The alpha rose up Bellamy's body, planting himself between two trembling thighs. He hefted both of Bellamy's legs onto his shoulders and angled his cock toward the slick hole ready and waiting to be filled.

"You want me inside you?"

"Yessss…" Bellamy cried, his head falling back on the pillows.

Quinn thrust forward, impaling Bellamy on the thick shaft. A moan tore from his lips, and another came right behind it. The alpha sank into his wet heat, growling deep in his throat. After a momentary pause, they went at it like beasts. After all, they weren't much more than animals, enslaved to their carnal desires.

"Harder!" Bellamy cried, his fingertips digging into Quinn's firm ass.

Quinn ignored his plea, holding back.

"Harder!" he screamed again, lifting his hips to meet the thrusts of the alpha's cock.

"No!" Quinn demanded, pinning Bellamy under him.

Bellamy hissed, angry to not get his way.

Quinn pulled out.

"Don't stop!"

The alpha grabbed him by one leg and spun him to his knees. Quinn's cock slid back into him from behind. Bellamy moaned and chuckled at the same time, glad to have his male back inside him. *Where you belong.*

Both of the man's hands went to Bellamy's hips, guiding the renewed motion and pace.

Still, it wasn't as rough as he wanted. He tried to push against Quinn's hold on him, but failed.

"The baby," Quinn whispered and it was then he realized the alpha held back… in case he was pregnant.

Bellamy scooted forward, coming off the alpha's cock. "I don't even know if there is a baby."

"I won't harm you… you know I can't," Quinn said before spinning Bellamy again and tugging him back underneath. Pressing some of his weight down on Bellamy, he smiled. "Nor our babe, if there is one." Quinn cupped his jaw with one hand. "Another week and we'll know for sure. If you're not… I'll give you the pounding you deserve."

Bellamy smiled up at Quinn, wondering if it was some hint of the protective instinct an alpha had for his omega. But with the scent blocker, it should be impossible.

Right?

"Until then… we go a little slower," the alpha murmured just before he slid back into Bellamy's ass.

Bellamy moaned, loving the feel of Quinn inside him.

Quinn captured his stare, and slowly began to move. The frenetic pace of just moments before was gone. The need was still there, burning bright, but they had to hold back. Let it burn. Quinn kissed him leisurely, sipping from his lips.

When he lifted his head again, Bellamy met his stare. It was as if the alpha could see through him… flawed and raw…

He'd never felt more naked.

Or adored.

Quinn caressed the side of his cheek before lowering his lips again. The slow, seductive kisses burned low in his belly.

"I want you to be mine… mine to protect. Mine to love," Quinn whispered. "Mine to *possess*."

Possess? Bellamy gasped, the words as seductive as any of the others. He fought the instinctual need screaming through his mind and body as it was, struggling to not become one more thing Quinn McCreary owned. Yet he was falling under the alpha's spell and didn't want to stop the descent, no matter how far it took him. "And you? Will you be mine, too?"

"I already am," Quinn whispered, driving a little deeper.

A tremor raced down Bellamy's spine at that admission. He wasn't completely sure it was the truth, but in that moment, he wanted it to be. He wanted them to be equals, both sharing one another. When the alpha's hand wrapped around the base of his cock and began to move, Bellamy felt his orgasm rushing closer. He'd already been denied too many times…

It hit him the second he felt Quinn's cock jerk inside his ass. The knot at the base of Quinn's cock thickened, locking them together. He shouted his release seconds before Quinn did. They came together, their cries mingling and bouncing off the bedroom walls. Bellamy's cum splashed on both their chests as Quinn filled his tight hole.

Boneless and panting, Bellamy was rolled to lie on top of the alpha, cock still planted deep. The knotting couldn't get him pregnant. Not now… not until he went into heat again.

Another heat. He quivered at the thought of days spent in bed with Quinn, his body sated after countless hours of steamy sex.

"You're amazing," Quinn whispered before kissing Bellamy's brow.

"I could say the same," he said, a smile on his lips.

He rested his head on Quinn's chest and listened to the rhythmic pumping of the alpha's heart. He felt his own shifting to match…

"I think we should get mated," Quinn said suddenly.

"What?" Bellamy lifted his head and frowned, sure he'd just imagined a proposal.

"I want us to mate. The sooner, the better. I want you to be my husband."

The immediate thrill he felt was offset as his mind spun. *The sooner, the better.* "Why the rush?"

"Sometimes you know when something's right. This is right between us. Even if we're not bond-mates, there's *something* linking us together. We can go to the courthouse tomorrow and make it official."

Red flags were screaming inside his mind. "Tomorrow? I'm not mating you tomorrow."

"Why not? You must feel this connection, too."

"I do," Bellamy admitted, still in the afterglow of another monumental fuck, but they weren't ready to dive into a mating. Not when Quinn didn't know the full truth. "But there's somet—"

Quinn placed a finger over his lips. "Throw caution to the wind... I want you... you want me. Why not jump in with both feet? Tomorrow, we can start our new life together."

Bellamy frowned—as he felt the knot finally fading. "Why do I feel like you're not telling me something?"

Quinn looked away, sighing. It was then, Bellamy knew he'd hit the nail on the head.

"*What* aren't you telling me?"

"Are you living in the Western Provinces illegally?"

Bellamy tensed and tried to scoot off Quinn, but the alpha grabbed both hands. "Is this what you'll do? I heard you'd be willing to do anything to get what you want. I see that's true."

Fitz had been right all along.

"No!" Quinn said, letting go.

Bellamy slid off the alpha and pulled the sheets over his nudity, suddenly at odds with the intimacy of moments before. "Then why does it feel like I'm being threatened?"

"Charles... he says if I don't mate him... he'll have you shipped back east and imprisoned in an Omega Quad."

Bellamy glared at Quinn. "*Charles* is doing this? Sure."

"He won't let go… and I won't see you imprisoned."

"So mate Charles then!" Bellamy shouted, the anger getting the better of him. *What am I saying? He's mine…*

"It's the only way I could think to save us both. I won't mate Charles… and if you mate me… you'll automatically have citizenship here. Charles can't send you away."

Bellamy was silent, his mind searching for ways out.

"I'm trying to save you!" Quinn added, filling the quiet.

"While saving your own ass…" Bellamy shook his head. "This isn't how it's supposed to work. You don't know me. Sure, you feel lust, but that's it. I want to mate with someone I love. Someone I know inside and out…"

"Most matings start off with just a little bit of lust. Love takes time. Which we don't have. It takes work… we can make it work after the ceremony, Bell."

"Don't call me that!" Bellamy crossed his arms over his chest.

"I only wish to save you… and our potential unborn child."

"You mean save me from the shitshow of *your* making?"

"I didn't do this. *Charles did.* Yes, I want to save myself from that hell… by mating a man I feel a connection with… a connection unlike any I've ever known." He sighed. "We might not be bond-mates… but there *is* something there, Bellamy. Tell me I lie."

Bellamy glared at Quinn. He didn't like being forced into doing anything... even if it was for his own best interests. But he couldn't lie. Not about something as important as this. "You don't lie."

Quinn lifted his chin, forcing his stare.

"Be my husband. Let me protect you... and our babe. Protect me in the process..."

"Charles," Bellamy scowled. "You have *some* taste in men."

"What does that say that I like you, then?"

Bellamy rolled his eyes. "The gods only know."

"Do you have a better solution? One where I don't have to mate that asshole and you don't get sent to a virtual prison?"

His mind spun. "I need time... maybe there's another solution." A rushed mating where the alpha didn't know they were bond-mates wasn't exactly the wedding he'd seen for himself. He wanted love. Romance. Not a version of a shotgun wedding where he might or might not be pregnant.

"Charles has given me little time, some of which I used up during my business trip. I don't know how much longer I can stretch this out."

The fact that Quinn was his bond-mate, he *should* just accept his fate and say yes. Yet there was something about Quinn rushing in, assuming Bellamy would just fall at the alpha's feet, thanking the good gods above for his savior, that just rubbed him raw.

Charles was Quinn's problem.

Now he was suffering because of that problem.

Goodbye independence. Goodbye autonomy. Goodbye career. Now I can let him sweep me up to his castle where I can pop out babies and wipe shitty asses.

What other choice do I have, though?

If Charles truly has the means to send me back east, how do I get out of this?

Where do I run?

Bellamy glanced at Quinn, knowing it was an easy solution to a difficult problem. *He is my bond-mate… and I could already be pregnant with his child.*

"I hate you right now," Bellamy said to Quinn, only half-joking. "Just know that."

Quinn smiled. "Love and hate… there's a fine line there. I think I have the power to woo you back to the other side."

Bellamy glared at the alpha. "Back? That's assuming I loved you in the first place."

Quinn swept his thumb over Bellamy's lower lip. "You feel something more than lust… same as I. It might not be love… yet… but I think there's a seed there."

Bellamy stared at Quinn.

Love. He *didn't* love Quinn.

But there indeed was something there more than lust. He *was* falling… even with the man's obvious flaws.

He's demanding.

Overbearing.

Assumes he'll have his way.

Quinn met his stare, a slight smile to the alpha's lips.

And he makes my heart shutter with a single look.

"I want to be with you," Quinn said as he lifted a hand to cup Bellamy's cheek. "I *need* to be with you. I don't understand this obsession I have… but the last few weeks without seeing you have been mind-numbing. I can't get any work done. I can't sleep." He paused, pursing his lips slightly. "All I can think about is you. Wondering if you're okay… wondering if you're thinking about me, too."

I have…

"Sure, me offering myself to you gets me out of a sticky situation… but it's not the only reason I asked you that question. I sense we'd be good together… if we gave it a try."

Bellamy stared into the alpha's eyes, the truth on the tip of his tongue. *I'm already yours.* He didn't understand why he couldn't say it. Eventually, Quinn would find out and then what?

More fighting? Every conversation they had seemed to devolve into an argument at some point.

Tell him.

Bellamy opened his mouth to say the truth, but something else crossed his lips, surprising them both.

"Yes. I'll be your husband."

Quinn grinned before leaning in and capturing Bellamy's lips. The kiss drew him closer, until he melted against the alpha.

Suddenly, Quinn pulled back and began to scent the air. "Is something burning?"

Oh fuck! Bellamy jumped from the bed and raced down the stairs naked. He pulled open the stove, just as the smoke alarm began to wail. More smoke poured out upon opening. Grabbing oven mitts, he pulled the two charred lasagnas from the oven and tossed them into the sink. Bellamy turned on the water and doused the smoke some before hitting the vent.

"I thought you said you could cook?" Quinn asked sarcastically behind him.

Bellamy turned and threw one of the oven mitts at the alpha, who caught it and laughed. He struggled to not laugh himself.

"Why don't I call for some take-out to be delivered? As soon as I can find where I dropped my pants." He paused and looked at Bellamy. "Giorgio has a good lasagna. How about that?"

Bellamy's mouth opened. Had Quinn figured out what he'd done? He turned and glanced at the trash. Apparently, he hadn't done a very good job of hiding the take-out boxes. Bellamy turned back to the alpha, his face growing red.

Quinn winked, phone in hand. He lifted it to his ear. "This is Quinn McCreary. I need two of your very best lasagnas delivered as soon as possible…"

"Giorgio's doesn't deliver," Bellamy murmured, but Quinn waved him off and continued ordering.

Thirty minutes later, they had a full meal delivered by a restaurant that didn't deliver.

Showing off how good it was to be a McCreary.

Chapter Ten

Wedded Bliss?

First thing the following morning, Quinn stood at Bellamy's side at the Province Hall, impatiently awaiting their witnesses to arrive. He'd texted both Beau and Tanner and told them to come immediately—it was a life and death emergency—but not to tell a soul where they were headed. Once his brothers arrived, the judge was inside, ready for the mating ceremony.

"Tanner's flaky. You know that," Bellamy said under his breath. "He might not even show up."

"I still needed to invite him. I haven't always been the best brother to him… and if he found out I mated one of his friends without so much as a phone call… I'd never hear the end of it."

From the corner of his eye, he saw Beau's head rising above the crowds. His younger brother was tall, even for an alpha, and could almost always be easily picked out of a crowd. Beau saw him and quickened his step. When he came to a pause before them, Quinn introduced his omega to his brother.

"Beau McCreary, meet Bellamy Carter."

Beau held out a hand. "Nice to meet you…"

"Likewise," Bellamy replied.

Beau's stare turned on Quinn. "So where's this emergency?"

"I need you to be my best man," Quinn murmured.

Beau's eyes widened, his mouth dropping open. "Ummm… *what?*"

"Bellamy and I are getting mated. As soon as Tanner gets here," Quinn added.

"Your plan to avoid mating Charles is to rush into a mating with someone else?" Beau turned to Bellamy. "No offense."

"None taken," the omega said. "I already told him this is crazy."

"Charles is holding something over my head… trying to force me to mate him." Quinn looked to Bellamy a moment before looking to his brother. "That something could hurt Bellamy. We mate, and it saves us both from hell."

"I'm sure there's something else that can be done versus a mating," Beau murmured.

"Maybe… but we don't have much time," Quinn said. "This is our only choice."

Beau wrapped an arm around Quinn's shoulders and led him a few feet away. He whispered his concerns. "What are you doing? Spur of the moment is not who you are."

"Maybe it needs to be."

"Do you even know this omega?"

"This is *the* omega. The one from the lake house."

Beau's eyes widened again. "Oh. You got your dick wet and lost your mind?"

Quinn sighed. "Him… or Charles."

"I'd say anything was better than Charles… but I wouldn't want to tempt fate," Beau said, glancing Bellamy's way. He looked back at Quinn. "How long have you known him? A few weeks?"

"Look… I know it sounds crazy. Maybe I *am* a little crazy for doing this… but what I feel for this omega is stronger than anything I've ever felt before.

I want him. More than I've ever wanted anything in my life."

"You said he wasn't your bond-mate."

Quinn frowned. "He said we're not… but whatever I feel… it's got to be as strong."

Beau shook his head. "What if your true bond-mate shows up tomorrow? Or his?"

"Then we figure things out at that point. For now… I just want to live in the moment. For once in my life I want to jump into something with both feet."

Beau sighed, silent a moment. "You sound like your mind's set."

"It is."

Beau nodded before turning back to Bellamy. "Welp, soon-to-be brother-in-law, how's it hanging?"

"As nervous as I am right now, I think my balls have shriveled up and are currently residing in my throat."

Beau chuckled. "That tense, hmm?"

Bellamy smiled at his brother. "Just a little."

"If my opinion matters *at all*, he's a good guy. Sometimes you have to kick his ass and make him do what he knows he should, but for the most part, he's a stand-up guy."

"So says you… who's even more a stranger than the man I'm about to be mated to," the omega said before eyeing Quinn. "We're nuts to do this. Absolutely and positively nuts."

"Think up that better solution?" Quinn asked.

Bellamy shook his head, frowning.

Quinn moved in close and cupped Bellamy's cheeks, forcing the omega to look at him. "We got this," he whispered. "I have faith."

Bellamy relaxed some in his hold, and he felt a stirring in his chest. He was falling for this omega who'd tumbled into his lap… an omega who wasn't his, but he was making the man his regardless. And if he was totally truthful, he was looking forward to having Bellamy as his husband… in his home… in his bed… swollen with his babies…

What in the hell has gotten into me?

Almost immediately, the omega had become an obsession. Separated from Bellamy, he'd floundered. He'd suffered day in and day out, unable to focus. Dreams had filled every night. Charles had offered him the perfect reason to lay claim to a man who shouldn't be his.

"Heeeeyyy!"

Quinn looked up and saw his youngest brother approaching. "About time."

"What did I miss?" Tanner said, looking between him and Bellamy.

"Nothing," Quinn said. "Follow us." After taking Bellamy's hand, he crossed the hall and knocked on the judge's door. A few seconds later, he heard a voice calling them inside. He opened the door and urged his omega inside and felt his brothers following.

The judge gave them a wide smile. "I see you have your witnesses."

"Witnesses for what?" Tanner asked, wide-eyed.

"For the mating ceremony," the judge answered before frowning. He turned to look at Quinn. "Correct."

"Yes, sir," Quinn said.

"Hot damn!" Tanner said before crowding in close and whispering, "Remind me to give you that painting as a wedding present."

"You already gifted that to me. Doesn't count," Quinn whispered back, just before the judge began speaking. "I expect a proper wedding present."

Quinn turned to face Bellamy, his face twisting into a smile he couldn't hold back. The omega looked up at him, his smile hiding some trepidation, it seemed.

We'll be fine… I know we'll be okay.
****

Bellamy's heartbeat was so loud, he feared everyone else heard it. The judge began speaking, and he barely heard the words, but a deep resonate mumble to his ears. He lifted his stare to his alpha, searching for something to anchor him and help him find solace. Quinn stared down, his eyes filled with a quiet strength that Bellamy needed to latch on to.

Quinn took his hands and held them tightly. Bellamy trembled at his touch, too overwrought by emotion to fight the tidal wave of lust he always felt in the man's presence. He still hadn't told Quinn the truth of who they were to each other, and the longer he held back, the harder it seemed to be to speak it. He'd tried the night before, but Quinn had silenced him, too stuck in his plans for their salvation.

After eating, they'd spent the rest of the night making love… and the morning had been a whirlwind preparing for this moment. A moment that was flashing by without him hearing a word.

"I promise to protect and provide for my omega… to care for him… to honor him… and to give him my strength when he requires," Quinn murmured, staring down at him.

"Will you take this omega as your husband?" the judge asked.

"I will," Quinn said with ease.

The judge turned to Bellamy. "And you…"

Bellamy searched his mind, looking for the mating words he'd long ago learned and now forgotten in the stress of the moment. Long ago, he'd thought to write his own vows, ones not so traditional as the old ones—but in that moment, he could only repeat the ones drilled into him. "I… promise to… cherish my alpha and submit to his will… provide a loving home… and give him the immortality of family."

Quinn dropped one of his hands, pressing it to Bellamy's stomach. He smiled, whispering, "You might already have."

"Will you take Quinn as your husband?" the judge asked.

Bellamy hesitated. He lifted his stare to Quinn and saw the moment uncertainty and fear bled into the alpha's features.

He wanted to be bound to his alpha. But not like this… not forced to mate because of a threat. He'd needed time… time to know Quinn more… time to know his life wouldn't change dramatically the moment he said the next words.

But there was no time.

"I will," he finally murmured and saw the relief flooding Quinn's face.

"Then by the powers granted to me by the province, I announce you husband… and husband."

Quinn's smile was infectious, and Bellamy couldn't help sharing it before the alpha leaned in to capture his lips. A hunger almost as strong as his heat hit him suddenly, and he kissed the man back, lost in that caress of lip upon lip. His fingers bunched in the front of Quinn's tux, dragging the alpha closer.

Applause circled them and reminded him they weren't alone. He stepped back, his face reddening as he looked around.

"Congratulations," Beau said.

"Absolutely! Congrats!" Tanner added. "We should go celebrate." He glanced down at his watch. "It's nearly lunchtime… you two should get something to eat before you end up in bed."

Bellamy chuckled. Leave it to Tanner's inappropriateness to help calm him down. "I could eat." He glanced at Quinn. "You?"

Quinn looked like he was ready to eat. But not food. The look of lust in his eyes nearly brought Bellamy to his knees. "If we must."

"We must," Beau said. "You don't get mated every day."

Bellamy took his new husband's arm and let the man lead him out of the courthouse. He barely listened as plans were made for where they'd go… he was so wound up, he likely wouldn't eat much anyway. He was urged into the back of a long, black car with Quinn and Tanner… and were off.

Bellamy sat between the two, feeling almost as if he were having an out of body experience. He was there, yet wasn't… and barely heard a word either of them said to one another. That continued through brunch. He nipped at the food, smiled at those there, and tried to take part in the conversation here and there…

By the time the celebration was over, and he and Quinn slipped into the back of the car alone, the alpha turned to him, concerned.

"You haven't said much today. Are you okay?"

Bellamy eyed him, not sure what to say. "It's been surreal… Yesterday I was Bellamy Carter with no plans of being mated. I had a life of my own. Now I'm suddenly Bellamy McCreary… and have to share my life with another."

"It's a bit late to have second thoughts now," Quinn murmured.

"I'm not having second thoughts… it just doesn't feel real."

Quinn turned his face, cupping his cheek. "Do I feel real?"

Without giving Bellamy a chance to answer, Quinn lowered his head and captured another kiss. The fire smoldering deep roared back to life at Quinn's touch… just as it always did. He soon found himself straddling the alpha's lap, and feeling the thick imprint of Quinn's hard cock pressing against his own.

Quinn broke the kiss and began undoing Bellamy's belt. Nimble fingers moved over the fastenings—without the shaking that his own hands would show—and soon his cock was in the alpha's strong hand. Quinn stroked him leisurely, from base to tip. Slick dripped from his ass, preparing him for more than a quick grope.

"Does *this* feel real?" Quinn asked in deep, hushed tones that set the fine hairs on his neck on end.

"Yessss," he hissed, arching his back. His head fell back, his lips parted as he panted.

The alpha cupped his balls and massaged them one after the other. "And this? Does *this* feel real?"

"Yessss."

Spinning, Quinn pinned him to the limo's wide, bench seat. Again, his lips were captured, a fiery kiss taking his breath away as Quinn's hand continued to work up and down his shaft. The need for release built in him quickly, the hints twisting in a ball low in his gut.

Quinn slid down his body, his mouth engulfing the head of Bellamy's cock. He laved up the drops of pre-cum before lifting his head a little. "Does *this* feel real?"

"My gods, yessss," Bellamy cried, thrusting his hips seeking more of that hot mouth.

Quinn wasted no time, circling the head again before sucking the whole length into his mouth. He sucked hard, hollowing his cheeks, as he feasted on the shaft. Bellamy slid his fingers into Quinn's dark strands and fisted it, forcing the alpha's head down faster. Quinn let him lead the pace for a moment before slowing back down.

He released Bellamy's cock with a pop. "What's the rush? We've got the rest of our lives."

Bellamy stared down at him, only growing lustier with the look in Quinn's eyes. "I need you. I need you to touch me... please don't stop."

"I don't plan to," Quinn murmured before returning to Bellamy's cock.

Bellamy watched the man, watched his cock disappearing between Quinn's lips... he lifted to meet the alpha's mouth... moaning as Quinn's stare met his. Moments after two thick fingers slid inside his slick asshole, he bucked on the seat—coming almost immediately. Quinn swallowed his cum, draining him dry as he cried out his release.

When the alpha lifted his stare, he licked one corner of his lips and looked hotter than sin. "That was very real, I hope."

Bellamy trembled in the afterglow of his release. "Very, very real…"

Quinn tucked Bellamy's softening cock back inside his pants and zipped him up.

"We're already over?" Bellamy asked, frowning. He was nowhere near being done.

"No… but we're almost home."

Home? Bellamy sat up, looking around. Outside the limo's window, he saw a huge cliff-side mansion all made of glass and metal. It was stunning… but he wondered if the inside would be as barren as the lake house had been. They hadn't had any conversations about where they'd live… how they would suddenly share a life…

And so it begins…

Bellamy knew that he'd slowly begin to lose himself to Quinn's world. All that was his would soon vanish. It would only happen faster if Quinn knew they were true bond-mates. The longer the alpha was kept in the dark, the longer Bellamy could keep a little part of himself whole.

As soon as the car stopped, Quinn slipped out and held out a hand. Bellamy took it and climbed out… only to see Charles on the steps to the house.

"What is he doing here?"

Quinn turned, frowning as he laid eyes on Charles. "He doesn't know about the mating... *yet,*" the alpha said before smirking.

"Oh please, let me," Bellamy whispered.

Quinn grinned. "Consider it my mating present."

Bellamy walked over to where Charles stood fuming.

"What are you doing here, omega?"

Bellamy felt Quinn sidling up behind him and immediately felt the man's strength. He focused on Charles. "I understand you were threatening to have me shipped off to the Eastern Provinces as a means to get your claws into Quinn."

Charles said nothing.

"What you didn't count on was Quinn's desire not to be mated to you... so much so that he mated *me* this morning."

Charles' mouth dropped open, and his stare went to Quinn. "You didn't?"

"Oh, I did. Well... *we* did," Quinn said, looking down at Bellamy. He lowered his head and pressed a gentle kiss to Bellamy's lips. "Hello, husband."

Charles silently simmered, scowling at them for a moment before collecting himself. "You will both regret doing this. Trust in that."

The beta stormed off, walking toward the gates.

As soon as he had exited, Bellamy smiled. "Well, *that* was a highlight of the day."

"Opposed to becoming my husband?"

Bellamy awkwardly froze. "Well, that, too."

Quinn turned to him. "I know you still have reservations... but I don't."

"It's kind of hard to not have reservations when you bring me here and call it home—without even thinking to have a conversation about where we will live together."

Quinn frowned. "But this house is larger… grander… it just made more sense. Here… let me show you."

They approached two large glass doors. He could see almost everything inside… and on out onto the valley below. The house itself was gorgeous, from what he could see.

As soon as Quinn opened the door, he lifted Bellamy over the threshold. "A little old tradition to start our new lives here."

Bellamy forced a smile. Quinn set him down just inside, and he got his first good look at the place. The metal and glass continued through. The whole first floor was basically open to itself, with the windows showing the mountains off to the distance and the valley between. Downtown, with its towering skyscrapers looked small and insignificant from there.

Just as he sees my life as small and insignificant.

Again, there was little color on the inside. Black leather couches and chairs set against the flagstone floors and foundations in the living area. A kitchen at the back was all granite and stainless steel, glimmering and looking nearly unused. A glass dining table was nearby. A glass staircase led upstairs to a glass balcony above. There was little art in the space, mostly steel figures on the stonework here and there. Like the lake house, it was a blank canvas—but then, the real star of the house was the outdoors which could be seen from just about every spot inside.

While beautiful, it didn't feel like an actual home.

"Isn't it stunning?" Quinn said, pride etched on his face.

"It's nice," Bellamy murmured.

Quinn's head whipped to the side. "Nice?"

Bellamy forced another smile, wondering if he'd continue doing that for the rest of his life.

"Let me show you upstairs."

Bellamy followed him up, seeing much of the same. As large as the house appeared, it was really only two bedrooms upstairs. Granted, they were both huge suites with their own bathrooms, but it wasn't as big as it appeared. Without walls, the house held an illusion of being more than it was.

Beautiful to look at, but missing much on the inside.

"I think you'll be comfortable here," Quinn said with a smile. "I'm sure you'll want to use your magic and make it more your own, which is fine."

Bellamy turned to eye the alpha, knowing he had to voice his opinions now or forever be rolled over. "It's a house you shared with Charles… cold… empty feeling… far from where I work… far from the life I lead."

"Your life is here now. With me."

Bellamy's jaw clenched. "Meaning?"

"You're my omega… our life is wherever we are together. Better?"

It sounded as if Quinn was trying to say the right words, but Bellamy wasn't sure the alpha truly felt them. "That works perfectly… *for you*. Not me."

Quinn sighed. "Should we move into your tiny townhouse together? I think not."

Bellamy took a step back. "This! This is the very reason I didn't want to rush into a mating with a man I barely knew. You assume I'll do whatever you want me to do. Whatever is mine is less valid. And let me guess... you probably want me to give up my work."

"Give it up, no... but you might need to scale back. Especially if there's a child to come."

Anger tore through Bellamy. "I won't give up doing what I love! Child or no child, I need to have autonomy. I won't bend to your will in all things, Quinn McCreary. I'm my own person, and I won't lose that because I'm now your husband."

Quinn stared at him, shocked. His jaw set into a firm line. "The vows you spoke earlier say differently."

"As if that mating ceremony was real!"

Quinn's frown grew even more. "It was. For me."

"I think perhaps we should remain mated in name only," Bellamy suddenly said. "You live your life... I live mine. All we needed was that piece of paper saying we're mated to protect us... anything else is superfluous."

He walked out before Quinn could reply and began to march down the stairs.

Quinn followed. "I want more than a mating on paper. And I think you do, too."

Bellamy turned at the base of the stairs and looked up. "You want a willing male under you... a submissive creature who'll do as you demand. I'm not that omega," Bellamy said, his heart breaking. "I'll *never* be that omega."

"Why must you fight me at every turn?"

"I'm fighting for my rights! For you to see me as my own person with my own needs! Needs you didn't even take into consideration."

"What about *my* needs?"

"All you've considered is *your* needs." Bellamy paused, trying to calm himself down. "The point is, you never even asked. We never had a conversation about our lives. This all happened too damned fast for it, I know. But now's the time and you don't seem willing or open to it. You seem to think I'll just fall into line and do as you say."

"I think you're simply being argumentative for the sake of it. I'm opening my life for you... giving you a beautiful home... a life and means well above what you have now. You won't need to work."

Bellamy winced. "Because you're throwing money at me and elevating me into your world, I should be grateful?"

"That's not what I said."

"It is... my life before I became a McCreary is inconsequential to you. Isn't it?"

Quinn looked down, saying nothing.

Bellamy turned and walked toward the door, ready to make good on his decision. He wouldn't be just one more of Quinn's belongings, placed in this museum of a home.

Quinn stopped him, pulling his back against the alpha's front.

"Don't leave me," Quinn whispered against his ear. "Please."

A question popped into Bellamy's mind. "Will you sell this house?"

Quinn scoffed. "No."

Bellamy closed his eyes before turning in Quinn's arms. "Being mated means finding a middle ground and making compromises. Since you don't seem capable of even considering finding that middle ground with me... I don't think you're ready to be a husband." Bellamy looked away. "And maybe I'm not either."

"You're willing to just walk away… Because I won't sell my house for you?"

"No… because you're not even open to listening to options… of finding room for me in this life you claimed you wanted us to share."

Quinn sighed angrily.

"I won't be one more thing you own."

"Fine. You want to go. I'll call a car for you," Quinn added, walking away.

Quinn had miraculously let him go—which made Bellamy wonder if he was worth fighting for in the alpha's eyes.

Of course not.

Bellamy was left feeling cold and alone, standing near the door.

The car arrived soon, and he was inside it heading home not long after.

He watched the outside passing in a blur on his way home, wondering if he was making a huge mistake… yet terrified that if he didn't stand up for his own needs, he'd lose himself completely.

Either way, he lost.

****

Quinn watched the limo depart, anger and rejection coursing through his veins. He knew Bellamy felt the bond between them. It was magical when they were together, their touch enough to set the world on fire. He reached down and adjusted the erection pressing firmly against the zipper of his tailored slacks. Even fighting wasn't enough to dampen the need he felt every time Bellamy was in the room.

But his omega was scared.

Quinn had already noticed it... and their argument only compounded his thoughts. Whenever Bellamy didn't feel in control of a situation, he started an argument.

He'd hoped that the powerful emotions they shared would be enough to hold them together. Lust wasn't enough. He knew that... but he had hoped they could find a path to more than the combustion they felt in the bedroom. Apparently, that wasn't to be.

He'd offered the world, and the omega had rejected him.

Rejection wasn't something he was accustomed to.

And it burned, deep in his gut.

A part of him had wanted to lock his feisty omega away in his bedroom upstairs. Pin him down to the bed until the man had agreed to stay. But that would've only fueled Bellamy's arguments all the more.

Letting him go hadn't felt like the right move, either... but what other choice did he have? Have him stay and argue more?

He marched upstairs and looked at the bed they would've shared... and then it hit him. It was the bed he'd shared with Charles. He hadn't even considered how the omega would feel about that. Glancing around at the glass walls, he tried to imagine him and Bellamy living in the house together and couldn't get a picture in his mind.

Had he made a mistake mating a skittish omega? The man had looked like a frightened rabbit all through the ceremony and lunch after. Quinn had hoped their little encounter in the back of the limo would've calmed Bellamy, but it only seemed to frighten the omega more.

He would need to find a way to cement their connection one way or another. One day soon, he'd have his mate back in his arms. Come hell or high water.

Chapter Eleven

The following morning…

Bellamy's stomach turned before his eyes ever opened. He raced for the toilet, slipping on the bathroom rug as he slid onto his knees and puked his guts out. Once his stomach was empty, he rested his forehead on the cool rim of the toilet, waiting for the nausea to pass.

When he finally rose, he wet a clean washcloth and wiped his mouth and face. Lifting his stare to the mirror, a whisper glided through his mind.

His stare went down to his flat stomach.

Oh fuck.

On the way in to work, he stopped into a pharmacy and picked up a pregnancy test. When he arrived at work, he peed on the stick and set it on the counter before collecting the vases of dead flowers and discarding them—feeling guilty that he hadn't found somewhere to donate them after all. Tanner slipped into his office, a grand smile on his face.

"I didn't expect you to be here today. Some honeymoon. My brother really needs to get his shit together."

"No honeymoon," Bellamy murmured, not sure how much he should tell Tanner. "I have too much to do around here anyway."

"Well, it was kind of a spur of the moment thing. Maybe you two lovebirds can find some time soon to go away together." Tanner crossed the room and grabbed one of the vases of half-withering flowers. "Can I take this one? It would make a great still-life."

"A still-life? That doesn't sound like you, Mr. Avant-Garde."

Tanner smiled. "It's withering… in a day or two, it'll be worse. Painting a vase full of half-rotting flowers is *very* much my aesthetic."

Bellamy chuckled under his breath. "Have at it." His stare went to the bathroom, wondering what the test sitting on the counter would soon tell him.

"Why so glum?"

Bellamy's attention turned to Tanner. "Hmm?"

"Glum… you don't look happy. Shouldn't you be happy?" Tanner pushed some of his long violet hair over one shoulder before sarcastically adding, "Omegas are supposed to be *soo* happy to finally be mated and protected by the big, strong alphas, aren't we?"

Bellamy sat down on a stool. "You do realize we only mated because Charles was blackmailing him, right?"

Tanner's eyes widened, and he set the flowers down. "Wait… what?" A smile crossed his lips. "I need deets."

Bellamy wasn't in the mood, but he'd already opened his big mouth. "I was born in the Eastern Provinces… I'm living here illegally… well, *was* living here illegally. Charles found out and told Quinn he'd have me shipped off back east unless your brother mated him. Instead, he mated me… so he didn't have to mate Charles and I wouldn't be shipped off."

"Because now you're a citizen through your mating to Quinn," Tanner said.

"Exactly. I just have to submit our mating forms and I'll be safe." Bellamy shrugged. "So, it's just a mating on paper. We're not actually going to live together."

Tanner frowned. "Who's brilliant idea was this? The not living together one."

"Mine."

Tanner sighed. "I love you, B. I really do. But sometimes, you can be such a fucking idiot."

Bellamy glared at Tanner. "Excuse me?"

"He's head over heels for you."

"Not even. He was in a sticky situation. I was a means to an end."

"He didn't have to mate you. Not at all. Nor would he have to mate Charles in that scenario. Did you ever think that he could've simply washed his hands of it all? Let you be shipped off and not mate Charles."

Bellamy met Tanner's stare.

"He mated you because he didn't want you to leave… because he has feelings for you."

"Quinn likely wants to see if I'm pregnant. That's all."

Tanner smiled. "You don't see the way he looks at you. And as a matter of fact, you don't see the way *you* look at *him*, either."

Bellamy looked away. "If I mattered at all, he would've been open to compromising. He didn't care that the house he wanted us to share was the one he'd shared with Charles… or that his house was too far from my business. Hell, he said I needed to slow down working… or that I didn't have to work at all."

"Well, I'll give you that. My brother and compromise aren't exactly on friendly terms. But then alphas aren't known for giving in easily."

"I had to stand up for myself. And he was unwilling to listen."

"And you needed an excuse to run away," Tanner said.

"Yes…" Bellamy said before realizing what he'd answered. "I mean, no. I didn't run away. He didn't give me a choice."

Tanner shook his head, lifting one brow. "Had you wanted to stay… I bet you could've found a way to convince your new husband to do whatever you wanted him to do. I get the strong sensation he would've given you anything you wanted."

"It's not like that."

"Hold on a moment," Tanner said before leaving. He returned a few minutes later, a frame in his hand. "Do you recall him asking about that gift I gave him?"

"Yeah," Bellamy said.

"He's obsessed with this painting… has been driving me nuts to give it to him." Tanner smiled before turning it around.

Bellamy didn't speak. He couldn't.

"He wanted this painting because it's you," Tanner murmured. "You should've seen him when I showed it to him the first time. He was… mesmerized."

"I feel sort of like that painting," Bellamy murmured. "A thing he must acquire. And it scares the hell out of me… because I don't know if I'm strong enough to have my voice heard."

"You sound pretty strong to me… and you've got my brother wrapped around your fingers already. All you have to do is let him in."

Bellamy stared back at the painting.

"But what do I know?" Tanner said after a moment. "I've been hiding from my alpha for years now."

"What?" Bellamy asked, his head whipping up.

Tanner smiled. "I happen to know that my alpha will *not* be happy when he learns the truth… so, I figure I'll just live out my life for as long as I can, doing as I damned well please, until I can't take it anymore and submit to the bastard."

"Who is it?"

Tanner smiled. "Better you not know." He turned and walked over to another set of flowers. "Maybe I paint this one instead."

Changing the subject? Oh no… "You don't get off that easy."

Tanner grinned. "One day I might share that with you… but I think I need to see that an alpha and omega can overcome the odds and find happiness first."

Bellamy lifted an eyebrow and glared at Tanner, deciding it was his turn to change the subject. "Take both vases. You can decide which one is rotting better before you paint them."

"Good idea," Tanner said before setting it down. "Let me hit the bathroom before I go."

"No!" Bellamy said, jumping from the stool.

Tanner eyed him, smiling. "You got a dead body in there?"

"Of course not," Bellamy said… searching for a reason to keep Tanner out.

Before he could come up with something, Tanner raced toward the bathroom and lifted the pee stick before Bellamy could get it out of his hands.

"Ohhhh, I *will* be getting a nephew, it seems," Tanner said before handing it over. "It's wet."

"I peed on it," Bellamy said, smugly.

Tanner looked at his hand, cringing.

"Serves you right," Bellamy said.

Tanner turned and washed his hands off. "You will tell him, won't you?"

Bellamy looked down at the stick and sighed. "Yes." He lifted his stare to Tanner. "Eventually."

"He *should* know."

"I'll tell him. I promise," Bellamy said. "Just give me some time."

"I think I'll just hold it until I go upstairs now." He dried off his hands, scooped his two vases of flowers up, and left with a nod.

Bellamy looked back down at the two little lines and knew his life was truly flipped upside down at that point. He would have to tell Quinn…

He sat back down, considering Tanner's comments. Quinn *could've* washed his hands. He could've let Bellamy be shipped off and put behind prison walls. Yet he hadn't.

Bellamy had been so wrapped up in holding on to the life he already had that he'd argued with Quinn for doing the same damned thing. Neither of them were ready to be mated, truth be told. He glanced down at his stomach and knew he would have to concede. Eventually. He still had a few months of freedom before he began to show.

Time enough to wrap up a few last jobs and wind down. A last hurrah, of sorts.

And then he could submit to his alpha, as the gods intended.

One Wild Heat

****

"Morning! I didn't expect you here today."

Quinn lifted his stare from a report on his computer to eye Beau. "It's a workday, just like any other."

"But you were just mated yesterday."

Quinn scowled. "So I was."

Beau's smile faded. "Already trouble at home?"

"That's none of your business," Quinn spat.

Beau lifted both hands in mock surrender. "You got it… Your problems are your own, but I'm really not surprised. I mean, what did I expect when my brother mated a virtual stranger out of nowhere?"

"Get out of my office," Quinn growled. "Before I say something you won't like."

Beau chuckled. "Have fun stewing in here. Alone."

His brother left quickly, fortunately. Quinn had gotten through most of the morning before he was summoned to his grandfather's office. His grandfather looked furious, seated behind his huge desk.

"Were you ignoring me, Quinn?"

"Not at all," he answered, trying to rein in the foul mood he was in before he took his grandfather's head off.

"Sorry that your strategy to discredit me backfired?"

Quinn frowned. *What the hell is he talking about?* "My strategy to discredit you?"

"Beau dragged me to see a doctor while you were away—apparently under your orders. I'm as fit as a fiddle. I'm sure he's shared that with you."

He knew I was sending him to see a doctor. We discussed it. "He only took you to see your GP. Now we need to get a specialist. Someone who focuses in cognition and memory."

"Cognition?" Tolliver sputtered. "I'm as clear minded today as I was at thirty. No more doctors."

"I know about the dementia, Grandfather. I also know you demanded your assistant not tell us."

Tolliver's face grew deep red. "I did no such thing! You want your hands on my company, and it'll be over my dead body. Not a moment before."

Quinn shook his head. "I was looking out for your welfare. That's *all*."

"Lies! I built this company from the ground up, and I won't have you stealing it out from under me! Who do you think you're playing with? I can ruin you!"

"Ruin me?" Quinn rose from the chair, rage filling him. "Ruin me…" He shook his head. "Fine… if you're so fit and clear-minded, then you don't need me. Keep your company… I don't want it. I quit." Quinn spun and started walking out, but paused and turned back. "And another thing… your plan with Charles backfired, I'm sorry to say."

"What plan?" Tolliver asked.

"I mated Bellamy Carter yesterday. Well, he's Bellamy *McCreary* now." Quinn paused a moment, wondering if he wasn't setting himself up to fail. He shouldn't crow so loudly when his omega wasn't technically his…

His grandfather shook his head. "You walk away from a wealthy beta… marry a poor omega… and then quit your job as the head of this company. Stupid fool."

"Am I the head, though? I wasn't, not truly… and I *am* a McCreary. We're known for falling down and getting back up again, only to climb to new heights. I'll find my own way in this world, Grandfather. Of that, I have no doubt."

He turned back and stalked out, ignoring his grandfather's commands for him to return. But as soon as he stalked into his office, he knew he'd been an asshole. His anger over Bellamy's rejection had fueled a foul mood all morning. It had allowed him to fly off the handle and say things he didn't mean.

Before that omega, he'd been cool and collected. Maybe Tolliver had been right about passion after all. It was already turning his world upside down.

His assistant raced in moments later, his face pale. "Your grandfather—"

"I'll go up and talk to him in a minute… after I've cooled down."

"He collapsed," his assistant continued. "They've called for the medics."

Fuck!

Quinn raced back to his grandfather's office, terrified of what he'd find.

****

St. Vincent's Hospital

Bellamy adjusted the tray and bags of food in his hands as he exited the third-floor elevator. He'd heard on the news that Tolliver McCreary was rushed in and was in the ICU on television. After a few texts to Tanner, he'd gotten some additional info. The whole family was encamped in a waiting room, hoping the old man pulled through—including Quinn.

He followed the signs toward the waiting area, hoping his being there wouldn't be too out of place. As soon as he rounded one corner, he came face to face with his husband.

"You're here…"

Bellamy's face heated. He looked down at the tray. "I thought you all might like some coffee… and something to eat." He lifted his arms some. "I brought a carafe, cups, and assorted items. Along with some donuts, bagels, and fruit. It's not much, but I wanted to help in some way."

Quinn began taking some of the bags from him and smiled. "I appreciate you coming. You didn't have to."

"You're my mate. These are the things we're supposed to do for one another, right?"

Quinn captured his stare. "I don't know… what are the things we're supposed to do for one another in a mating on paper?"

Bellamy froze, remaining silent.

"Sorry," Quinn muttered. "I didn't mean to be the one to start an argument. I've had little sleep the last few days, and my patience is thin."

"I did kind of deserve that."

Quinn chuckled. Slowly, he lifted his stare back to Bellamy's. They stood there a moment, not speaking, yet saying so much.

"Are you going to let him bring those in?" Tanner cried from inside the waiting room. "Don't bogart the Star Horton's coffee, Quinn!"

They both laughed at Tanner, and Quinn moved to the side to escort Bellamy in. Once they'd set everything up, Quinn introduced him to a few cousins, other assorted family and friends. "This is my... *friend*... Bellamy."

Bellamy tensed, unsure why he felt saddened that Quinn hadn't introduced him as more. *Mated on paper only.*

"Friend?" Tanner spoke up. "I thought he was your husband?"

Many eyes turned in their direction.

"Which is it, Quinn?" one of the cousins asked.

Quinn eyed Bellamy a moment before looking out to them. "Husband. He's my husband."

"When did this happen?" another cousin asked. "Does this mean Charles is free?"

"Yes, Hagar... Charles is all yours."

Hagar jumped up, reaching for his phone as he exited the waiting room.

"Is that *the* cousin?" Bellamy asked under his breath.

"It is," Quinn murmured.

"Charles really went bargain-barrel, didn't he?"

Quinn turned to face him and moved in close. "Does that mean you think I'm more handsome?" The alpha lifted his chin arrogantly.

Bellamy felt his face flaming. "Perhaps."

Quinn slid a hand along Bellamy's hip and drew him closer. "I've missed you."

"How can you miss what you never had?"

Quinn lowered his head, his lips beside Bellamy's ear. "Oh… I think we both know I've had it. And how much we both liked it…"

A tremor zipped down Bellamy's spine, heat firing in his gut.

"Will you two get a room?" Tanner cried.

Bellamy took a step back and glared at Tanner, who lifted a coffee cup and saluted him. "Thanks for the good java. This hospital's coffee is like mud." Tanner took a sip and smiled. "So what's new with you, Bellamy? Any news you'd like to share?"

"*No*," he grit between his teeth.

"Ah," Tanner said. "That's too bad."

"What's too bad?" Beau said, appearing in the entrance of the waiting room.

"Nothing," Tanner said, scowling. He lifted his cup. "But Bellamy *did* bring us sustenance."

"Huzzah!" Beau cried before walking closer. He leaned in for a hug, paused, backed off, and then offered a hand. "Not sure where we are in this relationship of ours, brother-in-law."

Bellamy chuckled and shook Beau's hand. "Either would've been fine."

"Noted for next time," Beau said before eyeing the small spread. "Star Horton's… I think I love you, Bellamy McCreary."

Bellamy froze a moment. No one had used his new moniker yet, other than himself, and hearing it sounded so… *weird*. Yet joyful at the same time. He turned to see Quinn staring at him, an odd look to the man's face.

"How's your grandfather?" he asked, trying to push down the heat bubbling in his gut.

Quinn frowned. "He had a massive heart attack. They rushed him into double bypass surgery, so now we're just waiting to see if he can recover from it."

"Has he awakened at all?"

"Here and there," Beau added. "It's only for brief moments, and he doesn't seem to be fully aware of what's going on."

"What's the prognosis?" Bellamy asked.

"At this point, it's just a wait and see. With his age…" Quinn paused. "We don't know. The doctors hope he'll come around more in the next couple of days."

"I'll keep him in my prayers," Bellamy said.

"Thank you," Quinn said, taking Bellamy's hands in his.

Bellamy lifted his stare to his alpha's and felt another wave of heat hit him. It wasn't the time nor the place for his lusts. He began to pull his hands away. "I should go. I just wanted to stop in and check on you all."

"You don't have to go," Quinn said, capturing one of Bellamy's hands in his grip.

Bellamy hesitated.

"Take a walk with me," Quinn said, pulling Bellamy's hand.

Bellamy nodded.

They left the waiting room and the stares of the family behind. Quinn was quiet at his side as they walked… leading him into a small chapel on the other side of the hospital. The alpha sat on one of the pews and urged Bellamy to sit beside him.

The chapel was darker… quiet. They were all alone, surrounded by numerous religious symbols and statues. There was a peacefulness there…

"It's my fault," Quinn said softly. He stared down at Bellamy's hand held tight between both of his. He lifted his stare and met Bellamy's. "My grandfather's heart attack. I did it to him."

"You can't blame yourself if he had health issues."

Quinn sat back in the pew, a pensive look on his face. "I told you he'd wanted me to mate Charles."

"You did."

"I'd told him I mated you... right after telling him I quit."

"You quit?" Bellamy asked, frowning.

"Long story short, he's been having memory issues... I had Beau take him to see a doctor. He was livid... we argued... he claimed to be healthy and that I was trying to steal his company... so I quit... and on the way out, I added the second gut-punch, telling him about you. Not long after, they found him collapsed on the floor of his office." He eyed Bellamy. "So yeah... I did this."

"You don't know that."

"I do," Quinn murmured. "I was so angry in that moment, I wasn't thinking about him. I was upset... hadn't slept... I lashed out at him when I knew better. By the time I got back to my office I realized my reaction was infantile, at best."

Bellamy was thoughtful a moment. "*When* did he have his heart attack?"

"Three days ago."

"Right after I walked out... leaving you angry. So was this anger you felt because of me? Which you then unloaded on him?"

Quinn eyed him, silent.

"So, I suppose I'm partially to blame, too."

"No," Quinn said. "You're *not* to blame. I am. I take full responsibility for this."

Bellamy couldn't stop himself. He brushed some of Quinn's hair from his face and cupped the man's bearded cheek. "You don't know that your argument caused this. You both could've been talking jovially and it still happened. There's no reason to blame yourself."

"Easier said than done," Quinn answered, giving a wry smile.

"True."

Quinn lifted Bellamy's hand to his mouth and pressed a gentle kiss there. He chuckled. "The first thought out of my mind after quitting was I'd need capital in order to start a new business... and maybe I should just sell that fucking house and make my omega happy."

Bellamy smiled, feeling sad that he'd run so quickly. "I shouldn't have left you like that. I was afraid..."

"Of being one more of my possessions. You said." Quinn smiled slightly. "You weren't completely wrong. I did want to possess you... but not exactly in the way you think."

"There's a good way to be possessed?"

"There has to be... because you've possessed me from the moment you first set eyes on me. And the hell if I want it to stop."

Bellamy gasped at Quinn's words.

Quinn lifted a hand to cup Bellamy's cheek before stealing a kiss he felt soul deep.

When it was over, Bellamy felt his world spinning.

"I know everything happened too fast… crazily so. Maybe we reset everything and start over."

Bellamy tilted his head. "Start over?"

Quinn smiled. "Once my grandfather's out of the woods and I'm on level footing again… we go out on a date. You continue to live in your house, I'll live in mine… and we learn who one another is. I learn what makes you tick and vice versa. No sex. At least, not until we figure out we're ready for that again. Maybe then we can learn how to be better husbands."

Bellamy smiled. "I think that would be wonderful." He wasn't sure how he felt about the no sex part, but at least he didn't have to worry about going into heat in the near future. That thought gave Bellamy pause. Was it the right time to tell Quinn he was pregnant?

With his grandfather and talks of starting back over… maybe it was better he wait a bit.

"Good," Quinn whispered before leaning in for another kiss. He leaned back after and smiled. "At least *something* is going right today."

"What happens with the company… now that you quit?"

Quinn smiled. "Only my grandfather knew about that. I've been going in for a few hours each day to keep things in motion. As has Beau. Between us, we're keeping an eye on things."

"So no quitting and no selling of the house."

"Not yet," Quinn answered. "Things might change down the road, though. Who knows?"

Bellamy smiled. "You do realize it wasn't exactly about the house, right? Because that house is stunning. I would love to decorate it."

"Decorate it? The view is all the decoration it needs."

"True, but there are little touches that could've made it feel less like a museum and more a home," Bellamy said.

Quinn grinned. "We'll make our home somewhere else. Together. Wherever you want. For now, it's where I'll lay my head until I'm done wooing you."

"Wooing me? Oh boy."

Quinn laughed. He sat back and squeezed Bellamy's hand again. "I love how easily I can laugh when you're around." He chuckled. "Hell, even the arguments we get in are more emotion than I've felt with someone in my life." Quinn eyed him. "Passion. I once told my grandfather that's what I wanted… and I sense I'll have that with you."

"You already do, it seems."

Quinn's smile widened. "I should get back and check to see if anything's changed."

"Of course. I have a shipment coming in this afternoon for a house I'm working on not far from yours. I should get into the office."

They both rose. Quinn turned to him, cupping the back of his head. The kiss was one that was hard to walk away from.

But somehow they did…

Knowing the promise of another was there.

Bellamy soon arrived at his office and checked his voicemail.

"Mr. Carter, this is Howard Taft. I'm afraid we won't be needing your services after all. I expect the deposit to be returned immediately. Have a good day."

Shit… The shipment coming in later that day was for the Taft House. *What in the hell am I going to do with fifty rolls of that god-awful wallpaper Howard wanted for his bedroom? He's so* not *getting that deposit back.*

"Hello, this is Carron Kingsley. I need to cancel our appointment for next week. I've changed my mind. I think we'll wait on the renovations after all."

One job in progress, one he was trying to line up. Fuck. He hit the button to move on to the next message.

"Bellamy… this is Garret Stevenson. I'm afraid I've found another designer who understands my vision, more than I sensed you did… so, I'm afraid I'm firing you."

Bellamy dropped onto his office chair, almost afraid to listen to any more messages. He forged on and within thirty minutes, he'd lost four more potential jobs, another one in progress, and had two complaints about jobs he'd already done where the homeowners were demanding refunds.

I'm ruined.

Chapter Twelve

McCreary Towers...

A few days later, Quinn stared at the calendar on the computer screen, instead of reviewing the documents that had just come through from Barrington Industries. He eyed the date, his breathing growing tighter. The next full moon was almost upon them, and he suddenly realized he'd soon find out if his omega was carrying his child. An image of Bellamy growing big and swollen came to his mind, and he felt his body stir. Closing the calendar screen, he forced himself to return to the final sale documents. He was so preoccupied, he had to start back at the beginning.

As soon as he'd read and approved them and moved through his mountain of emails, he got a call from Beau to return to the hospital.

Tolliver was awake.

Quinn leaned back in his chair, realizing there was a chance he wouldn't be returning to the building. He looked around at his office, sensing he should feel a larger sense of dread.

But he didn't.

All he could think about was Bellamy. He wasn't sure if that was good or bad, but something told him that as long as he had his omega in his life, everything would turn out okay. He'd build a new life with Bell at his side. They'd forge a new path. Together.

Thirty minutes later, he arrived at the hospital and found Beau waiting for him.

"He's been asking for you."

He's gonna drop the axe on me. And he has every right to. "I'm sure he has."

As soon as he entered his grandfather's room in the ICU, Tanner rose and smiled.

"I'll let you two talk," Tanner said before leaving, his voice low and his whole demeanor very un-Tanner-like.

Once his brother left, Quinn finally got the nerve to lift his stare and meet his grandfather's.

"Hello, son."

Quinn took a few more steps inside the room and sat in the chair Tanner had just vacated. "You're still calling me that. Did you forget our argument?"

"No. I didn't forget it. I know my memory isn't what it used to be, but I very much remember that."

Quinn eyed the old man. "I'm sorry. I did this to you."

"You didn't," Tolliver said. "I pushed you too hard… and you pushed back. As any man would. I raised you to be strong… and to not suffer fools. I was being the fool. Not you."

"I think the world might stop revolving if it heard you say that."

Tolliver frowned. "Tanner gave me a little insight into your mating with Bellamy… and what Charles did trying to force you into mating him."

"You weren't a part of that second half?"

"No," Tolliver said, shaking his head. "You said you would make your own mistakes, and I was more than willing to let you make them and deal with the fallout of what happened after." Tolliver frowned and sighed. "But I did cross a line, too. I'm not completely blameless."

"How so?"

"I gave Charles a copy of your omega's file before you drew your line in the sand. It was already too late, but I didn't think anything would truly come of it. But I underestimated how ruthless Charles was." Tolliver chuckled. "Maybe he'll be a better businessman than I assumed."

Quinn smiled. "Maybe."

"I only wanted what I thought was best for you... and I ended up pushing you away. Just like I did to your father."

Quinn frowned.

"The accident... when you lost them... was because of me. Because I was trying to mold your father into a man he didn't want to be. So he left. Packed you, your brothers, and your papa into that car and drove off. They were heading east... they were going to start over there and give you boys a life without me."

"I don't recall that."

"You were barely five. Tanner was just an infant." Tears formed in Tolliver's eyes. "I thought I'd learned my lesson. I tried to do right by you and your brothers. When you resigned and walked out, it hit me. All the pain from losing your father..." Tolliver turned to him. "I was wrong to do what I did, and I'm sorry. So very sorry. I'll do whatever I need to in order to make it right."

"Apologizing is enough."

"No. It's not. I'll resign," Tolliver murmured. "And... and you can take over the company. I'm an old man... and I feel the years stretching me thin, Quinn. You should lead. It's your time, my boy."

"I quit, remember?"

"I don't accept your resignation. I need you, Quinn. I need you to take this company places I can't. Especially now. You were right. My mind's not what it once was. I couldn't admit it… but I won't let you walk away from your birthright. This company is for you… and Beau. And Tanner, if he ever decided he wanted to be a part of it—which I doubt."

Quinn was silent, considering all the things his grandfather had said.

"Say something," Tolliver whispered. "Please let me know I haven't ruined another relationship with one of my children."

"You haven't ruined anything. You've always been there for us, and I'm ashamed I walked away from you when you need us most. If anyone needs to be forgiven here, it's me."

Tolliver smiled. "There's nothing to forgive, Quinn. As long as you take the helm of this company and you do right by my legacy."

Quinn nodded. "I would do nothing less. But like you, I won't accept your resignation."

"Son… you need to run things."

"I can. I'm ready. But I need an advisor nearby."

Tolliver frowned. "I fear I might soon become a liability."

"This company *is* you, Tolliver McCreary. It's your sweat. Your blood. And your tears. I never wanted to steal *anything* from you. I had Beau take you to see a doctor only because I wanted to know how we could ensure you remained healthy and active for as long as possible. We need to know what we're up against and how to fight it. Which we *will*. In the meantime, McCreary Investments needs you as much as you need it. And *I* need you." He feared the minute his grandfather stopped having something to look forward to each and every day, that was the minute he began his descent. His title would change and his responsibilities would lessen, but they needed to keep his grandfather active.

A sheen of tears shone in Tolliver's eyes. Quinn had never seen them in his grandfather's eyes before. The old man took Quinn's hand. "After the things I've done, I don't deserve this."

"After the years you gave, raising the three of us, you absolutely do."

"I haven't always made things easy."

Quinn smiled. "Which made us tougher. More like you."

Tolliver nodded. "You're a better man than I ever was."

"Not hardly," Quinn murmured.

"Now… about this omega of yours. When will I get the chance to meet your Bellamy? Tanner seems to think you're quite smitten."

"Smitten?" Quinn asked, chuckling over the old term. "You know what? I am. I'm completely smitten by this omega."

"Who isn't your bond-mate?" his grandfather asked.

"He might not be that… but he *is* mine. I refuse to let go. No matter what."

Tolliver grinned. "You're *definitely* too much like me."

"You say that like it's a bad thing."

****

Later that evening…

Bellamy added up the meager amount of money left in his bank account and realized he had barely enough to pay his bills for the following month. He was on the brink of bankruptcy and had no idea how to find his way out. He had zero business… and nothing on the horizon. He'd spent the last days chasing leads and calling everyone he knew.

It was as if everyone had suddenly turned their backs on him.

He grabbed his phone and queued up Quinn's number, not knowing where else to turn. Just as he was about to hit Call, a knock came to his door. Bellamy rose and walked over to the door. Fitz leaned in the doorway.

"It's coming up to *that* time… I thought I'd stop by and see if I was needed."

Bellamy burst into tears.

Fitz quickly drew Bellamy inside and closed the door before pulling him closer. Bellamy melted into Fitz, knowing he shouldn't… but he was on the ledge and needed a friendly face. Fitz stood there silent a moment, hugging him tight and running a strong hand down Bellamy's back.

"Who do I need to kill?"

Bellamy chuckled and stepped back. He wiped at his eyes and shook his head. "No one. Everyone. I wish I knew who."

"What's wrong?"

"All of a sudden, all my clients fired me. My prospects backed out or fired me. I've got clients demanding returns of their deposits… old clients claiming things aren't right and wanting refunds… I'm basically inches from being bankrupt."

"*Fuuucck.*"

"Exactly," Bellamy said.

"Who did you piss off?" Fitz asked as he sat down on the arm of the couch.

"I think I know who… and I was about to make a call that I really don't want to make and beg for help."

"Then don't make it."

"I have to," Bellamy said.

Fitz grabbed Bellamy's hand. "Why don't we sit and you tell me everything?"

Bellamy tensed, knowing he owed it to Fitz to tell him the news… before the alpha heard it elsewhere. He sat down near Fitz on the couch, turning to face him. "There's something I need to tell you first."

"That you mated Quinn McCreary? If so, I already know."

Bellamy frowned. "You knew?"

"I knew."

"And you still showed up at my door, offering your services?"

"*My services?* Jeez, Bell, you make me sound like a prostitute."

Bellamy laughed. It felt good to laugh. "I didn't mean it like that."

Fitz grew quiet a moment. He turned and met Bellamy's stare. "I guess I held out one last hope." He smiled wanly. "Better question is… why are you here and not with him? He could help you with this issue, you know. The guy's made of money."

"Things moved way too fast… so we're going to start back over at the beginning," Bellamy said with a smile. "After his grandfather's condition improves and he takes care of things at work."

"Get used to it. Business and family always comes first for a McCreary."

"Hey now... *I'm* a McCreary."

Fitz groaned. "You're the only good one in the lot, then."

"Thanks." Bellamy paused. "I really don't want to go running to him to save me from this mess... even though he may be partially to blame. Well, not him exactly."

"He's to blame?"

"Focus, Fitz. I said not exactly. His beta... the guy he was seeing before me. Charles. He said I would regret mating Quinn. Charles could be vindictive enough to have me blackballed. I could see it."

"Already tangoed with him, hmm?"

"He lied. Said he and Quinn were engaged, just to get me out of the way."

"A real gem McCreary was dating." Fitz eyed him. "Even though it pains me to say it, you *should* call him. You need the help, especially if this Charles guy is the culprit. I wish I could help. I don't have that kind of extra cash. I mean, you can have whatever I have, if it'll help, but I don't have the kind of funds you likely need. And you'll always have a bed to sleep in at my place, but I doubt you'll use it."

Bellamy smiled. "You're too good to me considering."

"Considering?"

In the months prior, *Heatex* had begun to fail him. He hadn't wanted to go into a full heat—he hadn't had somewhere truly safe to do it. So he'd gone into a partial heat. Not enough to lose his mind, but enough that the lust had been intolerable. He could've taken care of his own needs, but Fitz had offered…

And a real alpha was always better than a fake dong.

Only he hadn't taken enough consideration for Fitz's feelings. More to the point, he hadn't expected Fitz to fall for him. And now he felt terrible. "I feel like I've used you."

"You didn't," Fitz murmured. "I offered. You accepted." He smiled. "It was fun while it lasted."

"It was."

Fitz grinned. "So… does he know you're pregnant?"

Bellamy's mouth dropped open. "Did Tanner tell you that, too?"

"Nope." Fitz eyed him. "Something I've noticed… mated omegas tend to avoid other alphas when they're getting real close to going into heat— even if they're on meds. Unless they're pregnant and know there's nothing to worry about." He tilted his head to Bellamy. "You wouldn't have let me this close now that you're mated unless you were pregnant."

"That sounds like an old omega's tale."

"It's instinctual. Trust me. Even my omega brothers back away from me when it's getting closer to that time. Which is weird and kind of gross."

"Ew. Agreed. You know, I've always wondered about families who have alphas and omegas in it… how do they avoid mistakes?"

"Oh, I'm sure it's happened out there in the world," Fitz said. "But I don't want to think about it."

"I was an only child… so I didn't have to contend with that."

"That's right." Fitz smiled. "I guess that mating makes you legal now, hmm?"

"It does."

"Well, there was something good that came from this mating." Fitz rose from the couch. "I think I'm going to head out… get a few drinks. Drown my sorrows *and* my broken heart."

"Guilt trip much?"

Fitz chuckled. "Hey, consider it my retaliation for you breaking my heart."

"If that's the worst of it, I think I can handle it. Much more and I might lose my mind."

"Call Quinn. Please."

"Maybe," Bellamy said.

Fitz smiled and kissed Bellamy on the cheek before leaving. Once he was gone, Bellamy stared at the phone, trying to get the bravery he needed to call his alpha and beg for help.

He tossed the phone aside. After all his cries that he wanted to be independent and didn't want Quinn's help, now was the time for him to put up or shut up.

I'll figure out a way…

****

A few hours later…

Quinn lay in bed, reading over a few reports. Bellamy once again came to mind. They hadn't spoken in a few days. He glanced at the clock. One in the morning. It was too late for him to call his omega…

A few minutes later, a buzzing sound came from downstairs. Someone was at the gate, buzzing to get in. He rose from his bed and peeked through the windows, but couldn't see well enough in the darkness. After heading to the first floor, he checked the monitors and saw the alpha he'd confronted in front of Bellamy's townhouse weeks before.

"Can I help you?" Quinn spoke into the communication system, holding the button.

"I need Quinn McCreary!" the man slurred.

"Do you have any idea what time it is?"

"Bellamy's in danger."

Quinn frowned and pressed the button again. "What kind of danger?"

"Buzz me in, asshole."

Quinn wasn't sure that was a good idea. Instead, he slid into a pair of shoes and stepped outside. He walked to the gate and stood on one side of it. "I should call the police."

"Bellamy's about to be ruined."

"Ruined?"

"Someone has gotten all his clients to fire him. He's about to go under. Bell thinks it's your friend, Charles."

"Then why didn't he call me?" Quinn asked, confused. Was this some kind of trick the alpha was pulling to get close enough to fight? "I could help him."

"I told him to call you. I hated saying it, but I said it. Then I saw it on his face. He's too proud. He won't call. So I came here for him."

"He told you about his problems, though." Anger simmered in Quinn's veins. This alpha had touched what was his… "He unburdened himself to you and not me?"

"Stopped to say hello. He burst into tears as soon as I said hello. I told him to go to you." The man scowled before swaying on his feet. "I hate being here right now… but I love him. I love Bellamy… and I don't give two fucks what you think about that. I love him enough to come to you… because you can help him where I can't."

Quinn wanted to go for the jugular with that admission. But he held back, sensing that love might be the only thing that saved his omega. He looked around, searching for a car. "Did you walk here? Please tell me you didn't drive?"

The alpha scrubbed his face with one hand and leaned on the gate's bars. "Nope… hitched a ride. I'm in *no* condition to drive, dude."

Quinn hit the remote button he'd snagged before exiting and opened up the gates. "Let's get you inside so you can sleep this off. Then I can go help Bellamy."

"I don't like you, McCreary."

Quinn chuckled. "I don't really care for you too much either. But there's no way I'm letting you leave in this condition. I sense Bellamy might hate me for it."

"You better believe he would," the alpha cried.

"You can go back to hating me tomorrow. Fitz, was it?"

"Mr. Fitzgerald Walker to you."

"Come on, Mr. Walker. Let's get you to bed."

Fitz begrudgingly accepted Quinn's help. He drew the man inside and helped him drop to the leather couch. After kicking off his shoes, the alpha lay down and Quinn covered him with a throw. He raced upstairs, threw on some clothes, and then grabbed his keys.

He had an omega to save.

****

Not much later…

Bellamy tossed and turned, unable to sleep when his career was going up in flames. He stared at the clock, his mind an anguished, chaotic swirl. His stomach hurt. His head hurt.

Everything else felt sort of numb.

He heard a knock downstairs and frowned. Again he eyed the clock. Two a.m. Bellamy crept down, fearful who would be knocking so late. He moved closer and checked the peephole.

Quinn.

Bellamy flung the door open wide.

"I hear there's a problem you need some help with."

Bellamy fought tears. *Who told him? Fitz? Impossible.* "I'll figure things out."

"Is that why you're still up at two in the morning? Trying to come up with solutions?" Quinn leaned closer. "I can help you. *Let me.*"

Bellamy hesitated… he didn't want to be beholden to anyone. "Come in."

Once the alpha was inside, he shut the door. "Who told you?"

"A very drunk alpha showed up at my gate, claiming he loved you and hated me, but that I was the best choice to help you."

"Fucking Fitz."

"Should I be angry that you told him and not me?"

"With your grandfather and the business, I didn't want to dump more in your lap. You have enough stress." Bellamy lifted his stare to the alpha.

"You're my husband. I vowed to provide and protect, remember? And if this really is Charles' doing—then I need to help clean up that mess."

"I screamed about wanting to be independent. It's the reason I used to leave your house. What's it say about me that I come running to you for help now? It would make me a hypocrite."

"More like too proud. You'd rather crash and burn than turn to me for help? Help you have to know I would offer in an instant."

Bellamy shook his head. "I'd rather not do either. I want to be able to stand on my own two feet."

"You were. Before someone out there purposefully set out to destroy you. You can't be expected to stand on your own in a situation like that."

Bellamy was silent, knowing Quinn's words made sense.

"How about we call it a loan?"

"A loan I could never repay? Come on, Quinn. That's patronizing."

Quinn smiled as he walked closer. He cupped Bellamy's chin. "Something tells me you'll soon be able to repay it in spades."

"Oh?"

Quinn nodded. "Indeed."

Bellamy rested his forehead on Quinn's chest a moment before lifting to look at his alpha. "A loan, then. If you don't mind offering it."

"I don't mind. Not in the least," Quinn whispered. "First thing in the morning, I'll have money moved into your account. I'll just need your numbers." He pressed a kiss to Bellamy's forehead. "But the banks don't open until the morning—so why don't we try and get some rest?"

"We? I thought we were starting back from square one?"

"Tonight I just want to make sure you get some rest. You look terrible."

"*Thanks.*"

Quinn chuckled before lifting Bellamy into his arms. "Let's go to bed, husband."

"Okay, husband."

Quinn carried him up, slid into bed with him, and cuddled close. Bellamy rested his head on his alpha's chest, letting the slow beating of the man's heart lull him to sleep. It was the best sleep he'd had in days. And when they woke up a few hours later, Quinn was as good as his word, transferring enough working capital for Bellamy to stay afloat while he considered what he did next. He spent the morning fielding calls from clients, repaying some deposits, and arguing with others about why that wasn't happening.

By the following afternoon, Bellamy stopped by his office to check emails and messages there. The first voicemail had him dropping into his office chair.

"Mr. McCreary? This is Alexander Quitton from the Provincial Minister's Offices. We received your name and contact info from one of our clients. We're interested in setting up a meeting to discuss a design change we wanted to make here at the offices, as well as the Minister's home." The man continued, listing his contact information. Bellamy quickly wrote the numbers and names down before answering another message.

Another one much like the first.

When he'd finished listening to his messages, he had six new major jobs possibly lined up. A smile came to his face as he realized every call had come for Bellamy McCreary. All his clients knew him as Bellamy Carter. He hadn't changed his name professionally yet, so he knew exactly where all this new business had come from.

He fished out his cell and called Quinn.

"Is today shaping up to be better?" the alpha asked after their greeting.

"I suddenly have six new potential clients."

"Do you?" Quinn asked. "See, I told you things would get better."

"Don't think for one minute I don't know where these clients came from. Do any of them really need me?"

"Trust me… I've been inside each and every one and they *absolutely* need to be updated."

"How much did you have to pay for them to call me?"

"Pay?" Quinn asked. "I didn't pay them anything."

"Oh?"

"I may have made sizeable donations to the charities of their choice, but I did *not* pay them one cent."

Bellamy closed his eyes and chuckled inwardly. The momentousness of the moment hit him. "Why are you doing all this for me?"

"Because you're my omega. And I want to be the man you turn to when you need help. Not Fitz. Not anyone else. Me."

Bellamy grew quiet. "Only if you let me be the one you turn to."

He could sense Quinn's smile on the other end. "Deal. By the way, my grandfather is clamoring to meet you."

Bellamy hit his head. "I didn't even ask about him last night. I was so wrapped up in my own mess." Quinn had texted him a few updates, and he'd checked in with Tanner a few times, and he knew the man was improving every day. But he should've asked.

"You had a right to be wrapped up in your own mess," Quinn said. "He's doing well. The doctors think he might be able to come home in a few days."

"That's great news. I'm sure that's a load off your mind."

"It is. Why don't we have dinner Friday night? Before we eat, maybe we can stop to see him so he can give you the once over."

Panic hit Bellamy. "The man who wanted you to marry Charles? Sure, no problem."

"He's had a change of heart. I'll make sure he's on his best behavior."

"Okay."

"I'll pick you up at seven? Visiting hours are over at eight."

"I'll see you at seven."

Chapter Thirteen

First Date…

The moment Bellamy opened the front door, Quinn knew there was no way he was making it through one night without his hands on his omega. There was something new about Bellamy, a look to him—a gleam to his eyes—some kind of change—something that was firing Quinn on the inside. He leaned in for a brief kiss, unable to stop himself.

"You look amazing," Quinn murmured as he pulled away.

Bellamy grinned up at him, making his heart beat a little faster. "So do you."

"Ready to go?"

"Yep," Bellamy replied before locking the door and tossing his keys in his pocket. "I finally get a ride in the little red sports car, I see."

"Assuming you want me to drive? I wouldn't want to overstep… in case you wanted to drive."

"Luckily for you, smart ass, I don't have a car."

Quinn frowned. "You don't?" He paused lifting his chin. "You know, I thought it was interesting that you had the same color, make, and model of my brother's car."

"I borrowed it for the trip up," Bellamy answered as Quinn led him to the passenger side.

Once Bellamy was inside, Quinn rounded the car and slid in behind the steering wheel. "How do you get to clients? Or deliver anything?"

"Most of my clients are in town, so I use the trolleys. I use a delivery company, or the manufacturers themselves, to deliver to client homes.

And if there's a client who's a bit out of the way, Tanner lets me borrow his car."

"You should have a car. Or a delivery van, at the very least," Quinn said as he turned on the engine.

"Maybe after all this business you've sent my way, I can afford to buy one."

Quinn pulled out of the spot he'd parked in, glancing Bellamy's way. "Is business that precarious?"

Bellamy shrugged. "It's a new venture. Living in a city with fabulous public transportation means a car isn't exactly a necessity. I've made it work."

Quinn was ready to buy a vehicle for his omega, knowing full well it would likely cross the line. He didn't care. He'd call a dealer in the morning.

"And don't be getting any ideas in that head of yours, either. I can already see the wheels moving in your mind."

Quinn glanced Bellamy's way and smiled. "I don't know what you're talking about."

"Liar."

Quinn chuckled and stomped on the accelerator, zipping through city traffic. Bellamy reached out and grabbed his thigh as they rounded a sharp corner, and Quinn stiffened a little. He stiffened somewhere else when that hand didn't leave his thigh.

When that hand began to slide in small circles over his leg, he grew rock hard.

No sex, hmm? Who's stupid idea was that?

He glanced Bellamy's way and saw heat in his omega's eyes before he looked back to the road, swerving slightly to avoid a collision with another car. "You'd better stop doing that or we're going to have a wreck."

"Stop doing what?" Bellamy asked, his hand dipping a little lower onto Quinn's inner thigh.

"Unfair," Quinn growled before he turned into the hospital's underground parking lot. As soon as he'd parked, he turned to Bellamy and dragged the man closer. "Play with fire and you might get burned."

"Something tells me I might like being burned."

Quinn kissed his omega, hungry for more. He slid his hand to the back of Bellamy's head, forcing them even closer.

A horn sounded down the row, reminding them where they were. As if they'd be able to do much in his tiny roadster, anyway. "Visiting hours aren't much longer. We should go up."

"I suppose," Bellamy said, his voice sounding deeper and husky… just like it had at the lake house.

"We'll revisit this, trust me," Quinn said before letting go. He nearly moaned when he saw the knowing smile Bellamy tried to hide.

They were soon knocking on his grandfather's door, checking to see if he was ready. "Let me go inside first and see how he's doing this evening."

Bellamy nodded and leaned on the wall outside the door.

Quinn peeked in to see Tolliver playing chess with Beau. "Good evening."

"Evening," both said in concert.

Quinn turned his gaze on Beau before smiling at his grandfather. "How we feeling tonight?"

"Pretty good," Tolliver said. Beau nodded, eyeing Quinn. "I'm just very ready to go home to my own bed."

"The doctor said tomorrow," Beau announced. "Tonight's your last one in captivity."

"For now," Tolliver said on a sigh.

"If you're up to a visitor, I brought someone you wanted to meet," Quinn said.

Tolliver pulled off his glasses. "Your mate?"

"Yes."

"I don't want him seeing me like this," his grandfather said, frowning.

"He's family now," Beau said. "Does it really matter?"

"Yes," Tolliver snapped. "I don't want to look weak."

"If it means anything, I don't think having a heart attack makes you weak," Bellamy said from the doorway. Quinn turned to look at his omega. "The fact you're still here means you're strong. A survivor."

Quinn looked toward his grandfather, who wore a blank expression. "You're here now, so I suppose you should come on in."

Bellamy walked in and offered a hand to his grandfather. Tolliver took it and shook. "So you're the omega who snared my grandson, are you?"

"I think it was a mutual snaring, if you want to get technical," Bellamy replied. "I'm still not sure if we weren't insane for doing it."

"Absolutely insane. But I've done some insane things that have paid off in the end. Whether this will or not, remains to be seen," Tolliver said.

"Only time will tell," Bellamy said. "You'll need to stick around a while and see how it pans out. Good thing you didn't die, hmmm?"

Quinn gasped inwardly at Bellamy's words. He looked at his grandfather, knowing the old man would likely explode.

Tolliver chuckled.

Actually chuckled.

"This one has moxie," Tolliver said. "Maybe he'll be a good match for you after all." His grandfather looked his way. "You wanted excitement… looks like you just might get it."

Quinn laughed, eyeing Beau. Beau looked as shocked as he felt.

They stayed a few more minutes before excusing themselves for dinner. Before they left, Quinn turned to Beau. "Barrington Industries…"

Beau frowned. "Yes?"

"If I'm stepping into grandfather's shoes, someone needs to move into mine. You ready to put yourself to the test with Barrington?"

"That's a huge deal."

"I won't turn my back on you. We do this together… with you taking more of a lead on the management side and trying to turn it around. How's that sound?"

Beau grinned. "Great. I'm ready."

"We'll see if you are, hmm?" He smacked his brother on the back and led Bellamy out of the hospital room. They didn't go far for dinner… just a small bistro around the corner from the hospital. Walking distance.

Quinn liked having Bellamy at his side as they walked down the sidewalk, the sun nearly set. The city always looked beautiful in the twilight. Bellamy looked beautiful in any light.

"I'm a little jealous of you… I always wanted brothers."

"An only child, hmm?"

Bellamy nodded. "My papa had issues after giving birth to me. He couldn't have any more children. I'm the one and only." His smile faded. "And I bet they regret that now."

"Regret? Why?"

"I'm only an omega. No alpha to carry on the family name. And then they sent me away."

"Why did they do that?"

"At first I didn't know I wouldn't be coming back. I was supposed to go stay with my grandfather who lived in Port Salem for a couple of weeks. I was getting close to heat age, and they said it might be my last chance to travel before I ended up in the O Quad. So I went, even though I'd never met my grandfather. Once I got here, they told me I couldn't come home." A hint of shine came to Bellamy's eyes as they walked.

"They kicked you out?"

"Yes and no. My parents thought I'd have a better chance here… I'd have more rights. A chance of more education. A better life." He paused, and they walked on silently a few more steps. "I wanted to go home. I was so homesick, but my papa convinced me to stay. He said it would be hard, but a life behind a wall wasn't the life for me. They gave up their own freedom to give me mine. I never asked for it… but I got it nonetheless. I think that's why I'm so adamant about holding on to my business and having a life of my own outside a mating. To completely surrender and lose myself would make their sacrifice for naught."

Families mean sacrifice. He turned to Bellamy. "Hearing your story helps make me understand why you feel so strongly. Explaining the why is a lot easier on both of us compared to arguing."

Bellamy's face twisted. "Sorry... it's instinct. To fight... not explain why."

"Something we need to work on, maybe? Communication."

Bellamy nodded. "You're right."

"So, you were raised by a grandfather, too."

"To a point. I was fourteen when I arrived. My grandfather—who was amazing—helped me finish school and helped pay for a university education. That's where I met Tanner, but we really didn't get close until the last few years. My grandfather passed, and I had nothing. Nowhere to live. I couldn't go home." Bellamy grinned. "I ran into Tanner, and he helped me out. Let me stay on his couch for a couple of months until I got a job." Bellamy smiled. "And then on top of that, he helped me found my own business when I got frustrated working for other people. We became great friends. I don't know what I would've done without him."

"Maybe I don't give my brother as much credit as he deserves."

"You don't," Bellamy said, eyeing him. "He's a good friend. You're lucky to have him as a brother."

"Here I have family and don't spend enough time with some of them—and you can't be with yours. Now that you're legal, are you considering traveling back east to see your parents?"

"I wish... technically, I'm still a citizen there and I'm not completely sure if my mating here would be enough for them not to detain me. I've called and

spoken to my parents… let them know about you.
They're still not allowed to leave the province because
they broke laws sending me away… so I don't know
that I'll ever get to see them again."

"That's a shame."

Bellamy lowered his head. They entered the
restaurant, pausing their conversation. After they were
seated, they were silent, contemplating the menus. He
kept looking over the edge at Bellamy. How strong
was this man? Kicked out of the home he knew at a
young age. Sent somewhere he didn't know and
expected to make a new life. Quinn couldn't image
his parents being alive and imagining never getting to
see them again. He missed his father and papa every
single day and would give anything to see them again.

"Here I am rambling on about me and my life. I
know a little of your past because of Tanner. I'm so
sorry for your loss."

"They've been gone so long that I have a hard
time remembering when they were alive. I was five
when they died."

"Wow. And Tolliver took all three of you in and
raised you."

"He did."

"He's more like a dad than a grandfather, I'd
expect."

Quinn nodded. "In a lot of ways he *is* my father.
Family's very important to him. A legacy. He talks of
it often. He lost all three of his own sons. My father
died in that accident. One uncle died as a child.
Another died from cancer when I was in college. I
can't imagine the heartache he's been through."

"Me either. I'd guess he has pushed you and
Beau to continue the family name?"

"Oh yes. It's all I've heard since I was barely old enough to have a mate. It's one of the reasons I was dating you know who. I'd once threatened to mate a beta if he didn't stop the endless introduction to available omegas. When he didn't listen, I made good on my threat to scare the piss out of him. It worked. For a while, at least. Who the hell would think he'd end up thinking the idea was a good one?"

"Who knows... maybe him suggesting Charles as a mate was him using reverse psychology on you. You did end up with an omega not long after." Bellamy grinned.

Quinn's eyes widened at the thought. "I wouldn't put it past the old man."

"Well, he might get exactly what he wanted sometime in the near future," Bellamy said.

"Oh? What's that?"

"A legacy."

Quinn frowned and smiled at the same time, trying to understand what his omega was saying. It hit. Suddenly. And he sat up a little straighter, a buzzing sound humming in his ears. "What?"

"Do I need to spell it out for you, Mr. McCreary?"

Quinn's heartbeat sped up. His mouth went dry. He nodded. "Yes. Spell it out. *Slowly.*"

"I took a home test. I should go get confirmation to be sure, but I feel quite confident that I am. I've had a bit of morning sickness already. Although it isn't always morning. Today it was the afternoon, but then my internal clock is all messed up right now."

Quinn felt his lips twitching into a smile. "You're pregnant."

Bellamy nodded a smile playing over his lips.

"You're pregnant," Quinn repeated before jumping to his feet in the middle of the restaurant and shouting. "You're pregnant!"

Bellamy smiled and nodded. Quinn rounded the table and dropped to his knees before he brought his omega into his arms. He captured Bellamy's mouth, hungry to savor the moment and taste his beautiful man.

He reared back, a thought hitting him. "I just sent a shitload of work your way."

"Yes. And I'm very appreciative of that."

"How are you going to get it all done? You're pregnant."

"I know I'm pregnant. And I can do the work just fine."

"You need to hire an assistant," Quinn said. "I'll pay his salary myself if I have to."

"I have helpers I hire on occasion. No worries."

"An assistant."

"I'm my own boss," Bellamy spat.

Quinn sighed. "Carrying *my* child."

"*Our* child, alpha."

Quinn smiled. "*Our* child." He leaned in and kissed Bellamy before lowering a hand to his omega's still flat stomach. Soon, that belly would stretch and grow round with his child. His smile widened, and he lifted his stare to Bellamy's. "Hi Papa."

Bellamy's lips twisted into a smile it looked like he wanted to fight, but failed.

Quinn leaned in again for another kiss, hungry to feel his omega next to him again. "Should we get dinner to go?"

Bellamy gasped. "This is our first date, technically. You're not rushing out. I believe you actually used the word woo. So woo me, husband."

"Oh, woo you, I will."

Quinn was fairly certain he lived up to his promise, as he got a sign.

After dinner.

After dessert.

After a walk through the park and the long ride home.

After Bellamy was lying naked and boneless against him, both of them panting with exhaustion.

"I love you," Bellamy mumbled seconds before falling asleep in his arms.

****

A few weeks later…

Bellamy pulled up before the huge brick estate on the outskirts of the city in the car Quinn had demanded he take. The residence was in an older neighborhood, one with homes that screamed of old money. There was green and wooded lots for as far as the eye could see, not a neighbor in sight—yet they were somehow only thirty minutes from the heart of downtown. Redecorating a home in this neighborhood could set him up for the future, if he did well.

He knocked on the door, the sound echoing through the house. When he met a beta at the door, he saw the space was empty inside.

A blank canvas. Bellamy felt like rubbing his hands together. *Goodie.* "Mr. Baskins? I'm Quinn C—

McCreary." He offered his hand. "We spoke on the phone earlier."

"Oh yes," the beta said, grinning ear to ear. "I'm so glad you've arrived. Come on inside."

Bellamy's scanned everything as he entered. A sweeping staircase railing made of heavy oak. Wainscoting. Perfect hardwood floors. A gorgeous chandelier in the middle of the foyer that looked centuries old. *This place is stunning even empty!*

"Would you like a tour of the place?" Mr. Baskins asked.

"Would I? Absolutely. This house is phenomenal."

"I'm so glad you think so," the beta said with a smile.

Bellamy pulled out a notebook. "If there are certain ideas you have, please let me know as we go through the rooms so I can jot down notes."

"No notes… we can save that for later. Why not just take it all in and see what's here first?"

Bellamy shrugged. He shoved the notebook back into his satchel and smiled. "Then let's take it in."

After touring the first floor—with its huge, professional kitchen, the study, the dining room, den, living room, salon, and sunroom, he was awestruck by the house. While it was most definitely too much house—it was everything he'd want in a home. A little part of him was so jealous of Mr. Baskins. Once they reached the second floor, he was even more so. Five large bedroom suites, one of which was the master— centered in the home—and they were enormous spaces fit for a king.

"Wow, this house is utterly fantastic." He glanced at the stairs heading to a third floor. "How much more does this place have?"

"A small movie theater… a library… a playroom for children. And then some rooms for the staff."

"Staff?" Bellamy glanced around. "I guess if you have a house this big, you need a staff to keep it going."

"I suppose so," Mr. Baskins said. "I believe the previous owners had a chef, a manny, and a manservant to help with all the tasks around here."

They climbed the stairs to the third floor, and Bellamy took it all in. This was how the other half lived, apparently. He'd never decorated a home anything like it. As they made their way back down to the first floor, Bellamy posed a question. "Since this is such a blank slate, I feel a little at a loss. Without knowing your personal style, I'll need to discuss things a little more in depth before I consider any plans."

"Oh no, I'm not the client. I'm the realtor."

Bellamy paused on the bottom step, cocking his head to the side. "Then who's my client?"

"I am."

Bellamy immediately recognized the voice. Quinn. His husband appeared from the study and leaned against the foyer wall.

"*You're* my client?"

Quinn looked to the realtor. "Can we have a moment alone?"

"Of course," the beta said. "I'll be just outside."

Once they were alone, Bellamy turned to his alpha. "What is this?"

"Hopefully… our new home."

Bellamy's eyes widened.

"It needs a little work," Quinn said. "It's a bit older, but that lends it some of its charm. Five huge main bedrooms. A nursery. A huge backyard for children to play in. Near both our jobs. A space for an office here if you wanted to work from home on occasion or the kids were sick."

"Kids? As far as I know we have one kid."

"So far," Quinn murmured.

"What happened to taking things slow?"

"You keep asking me that knowing full well we don't do slow," Quinn said, smiling smugly. "So what do you think?"

"About your comment or the house?"

"Either?"

Bellamy sighed. "We *don't* seem to be able to do things slow." He smiled at his alpha. "As far as the house, I need another full tour before I agree to anything." He was already in love with the house. He didn't need to see any more, but he wanted to see how well Quinn could sell him on the idea.

And he wanted to go through it again, envisioning him, Quinn, and their baby there.

They toured all three floors of the gorgeous house again. What work it needed was minimum, mostly a bit of updating fixtures here and there and some paint. It had room for a growing family, a family Quinn obviously wanted. "It's gorgeous."

"You haven't even seen the outside yet."

"Oh, there's more?"

"When I said there was a huge backyard, I wasn't kidding. A pool. A tennis court. A basketball court. A three-car garage… and there's still a ton of open, green space," Quinn said as he led Bellamy toward the backyard. "The best thing though, in my opinion that is, is the guest house."

Bellamy stepped out onto a huge deck on the back of the house and took in the amazing backyard. "And why is the guest house the best part?"

"It'll be perfect for the in-laws to visit once the baby arrives."

Bellamy paused a moment, letting those words sink in. "What did you say?" His heart sped up.

"My in-laws," Quinn murmured. "They'll need somewhere to stay close once you have the baby. I doubt your papa will want to be far from you those first weeks."

Bellamy looked up at Quinn. From the corner of his eye, he saw the door to the guest house open. His head spun…

And he saw his papa and father walk out and into the yard.

Tears blurred his vision. He trembled as he looked at the two people he loved most in the world. They both had tears in their eyes as they looked at him, smiling. He raced over the deck and nearly stumbled down the stairs before running into their arms.

It was the best hug he'd ever had in his life.

After the tears and hugs calmed down, he stepped back to get a good look at his papa and father. They'd aged in the thirteen years he'd been gone, but they still looked just as he'd remembered them. He turned to see Quinn standing not far away.

"How?"

"Quinn pulled a few strings," his father said, pulling his attention back to his parents. "Cleared the red tape and got our travel visas re-instated. Then I was suddenly offered a position at Barrington Industries, so it seems we're moving to the Western Provinces."

"You are?" Bellamy asked, thrilled to have his parents close. Especially his papa, considering the months ahead.

His papa cupped his cheeks. "We are. So we'll be here to meet that baby of yours."

Bellamy felt the tears welling up again.

"All thanks to your alpha," his father said.

Bellamy turned to Quinn and threw himself into the man's arms. "You've given me the best present you ever could've given me. I don't know how to repay you."

"Seeing your face is gift enough," Quinn murmured. He caressed the side of Bellamy's face. "I want to spend the rest of my life making you smile like this, if you'll let me."

Bellamy nodded before his alpha captured his lips.

Quinn had given him his family back... and now he would give his alpha a family in return. "Barrington Industries?"

"Yes," Quinn murmured.

"Didn't I hear that name discussed with Beau?"

Quinn grinned. "A subsidiary of McCreary Investments."

Bellamy fought back more tears.

"Your father has multiple degrees in Organizational Management. He's taught classes at several universities and has worked for multiple companies, helping them fine-tune their management structures. We had a need for a man like that at Barrington after our acquisition. I know it's not right here in Fort Seattle, but they'll be a three-hour train ride away, versus stuck across the country. It's the best I could do."

"Best you could do?" Bellamy rose to his tiptoes and pressed his lips to Quinn's lips. "It's more than I could've ever hoped for. *Thank you.*"

"You're welcome, husband." Quinn took both of Bellamy's hands and kissed them. "And with the guest house, they can visit often."

Bellamy kissed Quinn again before turning to his parents. "I can't believe you're both here."

"Nor can I," Bellamy's papa, Joel, said, hugging him close.

Quinn walked closer to his father, Henry, and offered a hand. "It was incredible finally getting to meet you both. I'm so glad you're finally here." He turned a smile to Bellamy. "I'm going to get out of your hair and let you three reconnect."

Bellamy reached out and grasped Quinn's hand. "Do you need to go?"

"Need? No… although I'm sure the realtor would like an answer. I assume it's a yes?"

Bellamy chuckled. "A resounding yes."

"Good," Quinn answered before sneaking another kiss. "I'll let him know as I leave."

"Stay," Bellamy whispered.

Quinn froze, capturing his stare. "I didn't want to be in the way."

Bellamy laced his fingers through Quinn's. "You're not in the way. You're family."

Quinn was silent a moment before lifting Bellamy's hand to his lips for another kiss.

"I've heard about the Pacific seafood out here in the Western Provinces," Henry said. "I'm sure you both know of some great restaurants where we can sit, catch up, and get to know one another."

"Sounds perfect," Quinn said before eyeing Bellamy.

Chapter Fourteen

Three months pregnant…

The next weeks were rife with chaos. Between
Bellamy's parents moving, his new clients, *two* new
assistants that he'd begrudgingly allowed Quinn to
hire, designing the changes on their new home, and
being pregnant—not to mention Quinn's new role at
McCreary Investments and them trying to handle his
grandfather's illness and treatment—it was bedlam.
Yet somehow, they made it all work. Of course, they
didn't see one another but for a few hours in the
morning and a few at night, but it was the quality of
the time. Not the quantity.

They had dinner together every night, even if it
was late. They cuddled in bed without work being
brought in, no matter if they were behind on a
project. And they awoke in each other's arms… and if
they weren't exhausted, they made love before going
off to face the day.

One morning, an alarm went off on Bellamy's
phone. A reminder that he needed to take his next
three-month dose of *Scentex*.

After staring at the notification for a few
seconds, Bellamy swiped the message off the screen
with the flick of one finger, smiling as he ignored the
reminder. It was time to come clean… and letting
Quinn figure it out on his own was the only way
Bellamy knew how to face it at that point. He'd kept
the news to himself too long.

There would be no denials. There might be
anger, he knew, but he'd face it full on and hope

Quinn wasn't too upset with him for holding back the truth.

He walked into the bathroom where Quinn was in the shower and snuck in to join him. The alpha was quick to pin him against the wall, cock hard and ready for another round. "Hey, baby."

Bellamy smiled up at Quinn, wrapping his arms around the man's neck. He felt his slick growing thicker, coating him for that second morning round. *"Hey."*

Quinn kissed him, mastering his mouth, and had him moaning in minutes. The alpha knelt at Bellamy's feet, one hand gripping the base of his cock—before releasing it quickly and sitting back on his haunches.

"I can't get enough of this belly." Quinn rested a hand on the three-month baby bump. He lifted his stare, a smile in it. The alpha ran his hand over the barely protruding swell before pressing a kiss to it.

"Can we get back to the stroking and kissing? The morning sickness might rear its ugly head at any moment, so let's embrace the calm before the storm with a storm of our own."

"A storm you want," Quinn said before taking Bellamy's cock in hand. "A storm you shall receive."

Quinn lowered his head and feasted on his husband's flesh, seeming eager to hear Bellamy's cries of satisfaction. He didn't have to wait long. Never did. Bellamy cried out, spilling at the back of Quinn's throat until he was weak-kneed. The alpha lifted Bellamy's legs, draping them over his arms, and braced them against the smooth tile of the shower before angling his cock. "Ready for me, baby?"

"Yess," he hissed.

One slick thrust and they were made one. Bellamy clung to his alpha as the man drove into him, over and over. Stretched over his husband's cock, he cried out, loving the thick impalement deep inside. Water sluiced over both their bodies as Quinn pushed them both to the edge and back again. The minute Bellamy felt the swelling of the knot, he cried out, coming in thick waves. Their cries mixed together, bounding around the bathroom, as they orgasmed together.

"You're like a drug," Quinn said between gasps for air. "And I am *forever* addicted."

"That's the way I like it."

Quinn chuckled, holding them aloft until the knot faded. Carefully, the alpha released him and placed his feet on the cool, tiled floor. "The boss is gonna be pissed at me for being late again."

"Luckily you're the boss," Bellamy said with a smile.

They washed their bodies, Quinn finishing up first. He left the shower and Bellamy in it a few minutes. When Bellamy was done, he left the shower and dried off. As he exited the bathroom, he saw his phone in Quinn's hand.

"Did I miss a call?"

"I thought so. It was a notification about your *Scentex*."

"Oh? I thought I deleted that."

"You already took it?" Quinn asked, an odd tone to his voice.

"No." Bellamy shrugged. "I will. Later."

Quinn eyed him. His brows furrowed. "Let me go get a dose for you."

Before Bellamy could stop him, Quinn ran from the room. Bellamy dried himself off more, trying to work up the nerve to tell his alpha the truth a wee bit early. Quinn returned moments later with the bottle from the fridge and a fresh syringe. "Need my help?"

"I'll take it later," Bellamy said. "I need to eat something or it makes me a bit queasy."

"You *are* going to take it, right?"

Bellamy struggled to maintain the lie. He simply nodded and looked away.

"If you don't take it… your alpha might find you."

Tell him. Bellamy nodded again. "I know."

"And take you away from me," Quinn added, looking a little nervous. "Excuse me… he'll *try* to take you away. I don't give up easily. I *won't* give up easily."

Bellamy smiled, forcing himself to tell Quinn the truth then and there. "Actually… I wanted to talk to you about that."

"You're not going to take it, are you?"

"No," Bellamy said. "But there's a res—"

"Have you met him? Your alpha?"

"Yes," Bellamy replied. "And I'm trying to tell—"

"I *don't* want to know!" Quinn roared.

Bellamy closed his mouth, shocked by Quinn's sudden anger.

"Let me spend a little more time in this fantasy world where you belong to me," Quinn whispered. "And no one else."

"I'm trying to explain!"

Quinn held up a hand, his eyes shining. "Don't. *Please* don't."

"I *am* yours."

Quinn stared at him. "Until your bond-mate comes for you."

Bellamy stood there, shaking. Apparently, Quinn was terrified he'd be taken away—and his inability to speak the truth had caused the man more anguish than he'd deserved. After all his alpha had done for him, why he'd never said those few words, he didn't know. "*You're* my bond-mate."

Quinn's eyes narrowed. "What?"

"*You're* my bond-mate."

Quinn stood silently a few minutes, gawking. "You've known all along, haven't you? Since the lake house?"

Bellamy looked away a moment before he lifted his stare. "No… I mean, I felt a bond, but I attributed it to the wild heat. It wasn't until afterwards. When I saw you again, I knew."

"And you pushed me away, knowing full well you and I belonged together?"

"I was afraid. Afraid you wouldn't let me be the man I wanted to be. I didn't know you well enough then. Now I do. And I'm not afraid anymore. You're the reason I'm not taking another dose. I *wanted* you to know the truth."

Quinn said nothing. He grabbed a few pieces of clothing and his shoes and left their bedroom.

Bellamy sat down on the end of the bed, shaking all over.

He'd expected anger…

But not that.

****

Quinn was halfway down the stairs before he came to a halt. The last time he'd foolishly walked away from an argument, the other person had ended up in the ICU. He'd just been delivered the best news he could hope for in his life. Bellamy was his.

His!

And what was he doing? Storming off?

Am I really that stupid?

Quinn spun and charged up the stairs. He threw open the bedroom door and saw Bellamy sitting on the end of the bed, eyes shining. Racing over, he knelt between Bellamy's thighs. He cast his shoes and clothes aside and gathered his omega's face in his hands. As he captured Bellamy's lips with his own, he realized he would never have to part with this man… this omega… "I love you," he whispered against Bellamy's lips. "I love you so much."

"I love you, too."

Quinn wanted to be angry. He wanted to scream, but inside he was so excited he couldn't hold on to the ire. "Do you know how many times I've worried about your alpha coming to find you and taking you away from me?"

"I'm sorry. I wanted to tell you… once I was about to and you literally put your finger over my lips and shut me up."

"I did that?"

"When you were trying to convince me to be your mate. You thought I was about to argue, so you *physically* stopped me from speaking."

"Well, arguing *is* your thing. It was a good assumption on my part."

Bellamy nodded. "But you would've known a lot sooner."

"There have been two months between then and now."

Bellamy's face grew red. "Once I realized you would be partner and not my master, I was ready to tell you. By then, it had been so long that I feared your anger." He paused. "And I wasn't too far off the mark with that guess." Tears shone in his eyes. "I was terrified I'd lost you there."

"You'll *never* lose me, baby," Quinn whispered before stealing another kiss. "I only want to be here by your side. For the rest of my days." He lifted Bellamy's stare to his. "No more secrets. No more half-truths. We're honest with each other—completely honest—from this moment forward. Okay?"

Bellamy nodded.

"Is there anything else?"

Bellamy shook his head. "No more secrets." His omega's nose wrinkled up, like he realized there was something else. "Nope. No more secrets."

"What is it?" Quinn asked.

"Nothing."

Quinn lifted a brow.

Bellamy winced. "It's *not* my secret to tell."

"We just promised not to keep anything from one another. And here you are, already breaking trust?"

His omega sighed. "I'll tell you—as long as you promise to keep this secret with your life. No sharing, especially not with the person who it belongs to."

Quinn nodded. "With my life."

"Tanner knows who is alpha is and has apparently known for some time."

Quinn's eyes widened. "Really? Who?"

Bellamy shrugged. "That part I don't know. He wouldn't tell me." He sighed with relief. "Oh my gods that one has been bubbling low for some time now. It felt so good to let it out." His omega lifted his chin. "You don't say a word to Tanner. If he knew I told you, he'd *kill* me."

Quinn chuckled. "I promise. I wouldn't mess with your friendship with my brother like that."

"Thank you."

He leaned in and stole one last kiss before rising. "While all I want to do is stay home with my omega, I need to get into the office. I've got a meeting to attend."

"And I have a million things to do," Bellamy said. "The fabric samples for the nursery should arrive today. I can't wait. I've never decorated a nursery before—and believe this one will be the best one *ever*."

Quinn pulled on his shirt and began buttoning. "Of course it will. It'll be ours."

Bellamy grinned up at him. His smile faded some, love shining in his eyes. "I love you, Quinn McCreary."

Quinn leaned in for a millionth kiss. He was already planning a billion more. "And I love you, Bellamy McCreary."

****

Two weeks later…

Quinn rolled over, awakening slowly. A sweet scent filled his nose. As he opened his eyes, his stare went to the steadily growing baby bump Bellamy carried. He moved his hand over the swell, growling low in his throat. Pleasure filled him… as did lust.

Powerful lust.

He drew in another inhale, the sweet, delicious smell calling to him. It took him a few moments to realize where the smell was originating. Quinn lowered his head and drew in Bellamy's musky scent, the sweetness to the omega's fragrance new.

Mine!

Quinn moved over his omega's body, pinning the man under him. Bellamy's eyes fluttered before opening. He stretched under Quinn and smiled.

"I guess the medicine finally wore off?"

Quinn lowered his head and captured his omega's lips, drinking in the true taste and scent of the man the gods had put in his path. "Yeah, I guess so."

His animal nature roared within, screaming that he claim his bond-mate by flesh. He rolled his hips, rubbing his hard cock against Bellamy's. His omega's back arched, the scent of slick and pre-cum filling the air—along with that delicious aroma that quickly drove him to the edge.

Bellamy rolled onto his knees and lifted his ass under Quinn.

"Take me, my alpha… make me yours."

Quinn lowered his hand and felt slick all over Bellamy's cheeks. He guided his rock-hard cock and slowly slid inside the warm, tight hole. "You already *are* mine."

But this was different and he knew it. This was the moment he'd dreamed of. The words had mattered, hearing his omega tell him they were bond-mates. But now, feeling it. Scenting it… knowing Bellamy was now fully his… forever. He ran a hand down his omega's burgeoning belly, swollen with his child.

This was the happily ever after he'd wanted for them both… and never thought they'd have.

He drove into his husband, shaking himself. The lust that tore through him comingled with the love that grew every day in his heart.

Quinn withdrew and turned his mate around. They would look at one another, eye to eye, as they joined. This was the first true moment of their lives together, and he wanted to see Bellamy's eyes as they came.

There wasn't long to wait. Bellamy cried out, roaring his release only minutes later. Quinn followed him soon after, knotting up and binding them as one. They collapsed onto the bed, entangled.

"There's no running away now," Quinn whispered.

"The only place I want to run is into your arms," Bellamy whispered back.

Quinn wrapped those arms around his omega, refusing to ever let go.

Epilogue

Six months later…

"Breathe, Bell… breathe through the pain."

"I *am* fucking breathing, you big jerk," Bellamy spat before screaming again in pain.

Quinn tried to help his omega breathe through the pain, as the birthing classes had trained them to do, but Bellamy wasn't taking too kindly to any of his coaching. "Sounds more like you're screaming."

"You try pushing a bowling ball from your body!" Bellamy screamed again, his face twisting in pain. "I hate you right now," Bellamy said, panting between words.

"Nothing I haven't heard before," Quinn mumbled.

Bellamy squeezed his hand again, screaming once more. Quinn winced, the bones in his hand ready to shatter under that hold.

"Take a break. We'll get you pushing again here in a minute," the doctor said behind him. "Just keep up your breathing, Bellamy."

Bellamy was on his knees, upright and facing Quinn. His face was coated in sweat, damp tendrils of hair twisting this way and that. Quinn used a cool, damp cloth to clean his omega's face. "You're okay… we got this."

"We? I don't see you pushing a baby out of your body right now."

"No, but I'm fairly sure I have a broken hand at the moment."

Bellamy groaned. "Doesn't compare." He cried out again, arching his back. "He's not letting me have a break."

The doctor checked Bellamy. "No—he's really ready to come out. One more good push and you just might be there, Bellamy."

Bellamy met Quinn's eyes. "I can't... I can't do this. Quinn, make it stop. Please..."

"Yes, you can! I know you can!" He wiped Bellamy's face again before cradling the man close. "I'm right here, baby. He's almost here... you're *so* close."

"One more good push, Bellamy," the doctor cried.

Bellamy screamed as he bore down. Quinn could feel the pressure emanating from his omega's body. He held onto Bellamy's, willing any and all the strength he had be given to his husband.

"Stop pushing, Bellamy! I've got him!"

Bellamy collapsed against Quinn and seconds later, a babe appeared in the doctor's hands. The baby's scream tore through the air before a nurse took him from the doctor's hands.

"You did it, baby! He's here!" Quinn carefully helped Bellamy lie down on his side, and the doctor went to work stitching him up.

"I want to see him," Bellamy whispered, pale and exhausted.

Quinn brushed his hair out of his eyes before lowering his lips for a kiss to his husband's brow. "They're cleaning him up right now."

Moments later, the nurse came with their son, wrapped tightly in a yellow blanket. He laid the babe beside Bellamy. Quinn looked down at the male he loved most in the world… and realized Bellamy had some serious competition for that spot suddenly. His heart melted as he stared down at his son.

"He's beautiful," Quinn whispered, his eyes tearing up.

Bellamy smiled up at Quinn before turning to look at their son. "He is. He's the most beautiful thing I've ever seen in my life."

"Looks like an alpha," the nurse said with a smile. "Can't be totally sure yet, but he's not omega."

It would be a few years before they'd know if their son was an alpha or a beta. It didn't really matter either way to Quinn. His omega had survived and so had their son. That was good enough for him.

Later, once Bellamy had been returned to his room and allowed a little sleep, the well-wishers came through. Soon, their room was filled with happy family. Bellamy's parents lovingly argued over what their grandparent names would be. Beau and Tanner fought over who the better uncle would be. Tolliver was having a good day, fortunately, and reminded both of Quinn's brothers that one awesome great-grandfather would always outmatch a lowly uncle.

Even Fitz stopped in to bring some flowers and a balloon to welcome baby Carter.

Quinn looked around the room at his new, huge family and smiled as he cradled his newborn son in his arms. He looked down at Bellamy, who'd drifted off to sleep once more.

"You've had enough time," Tolliver said. "Give his great-grandfather a chance."

Quinn felt a glimmer of worry about handing the tiny newborn to his grandfather. His dementia showed no signs of slowing… and if the man simply forget he needed to be gentle, it could spell trouble. Tolliver seemed to sense his hesitance.

"You can help me hold him, hmm?" Tolliver asked, sadness on his face.

Quinn hated having put it there, but he had to protect the babe in his arms. After Tolliver moved to the small loveseat in the room, Quinn sat beside him and leaned close. They watched the baby sleeping, which seemed so silly just days before. Quinn knew he could look at their babe sleeping forever, completely enrapt. He couldn't stop looking at this beautiful thing they'd made together.

He glanced at his sleeping mate, a smile to his lips.

"Reminds me of you," Tolliver whispered. "He looks *just* like you did when you were born." He grinned. "Just what this family needs. Another strong McCreary alpha to help lead us on in the next generation."

"Carter McCreary. He carries two families into the next generation," Quinn said, smiling at Joel and Henry.

"On that note," Joel said, slinking over. "I haven't had a turn yet."

His grandpapa took over and lifted little Carter into his arms. "My gods, he's beautiful."

Henry rose and stood looking over Joel's shoulder, beaming with pride. "Our first grandbaby." He looked to Quinn. "Hopefully there's more to come."

"If I can convince your son, yes."

"I'm *not* going through this again any time soon," Bellamy murmured weakly.

Quinn gave his grandfather a squeeze before rising and carefully sliding into the hospital bed beside his husband. Bellamy snuggled in close, resting his head on Quinn's shoulder.

"You did good," Quinn whispered.

"I hate you less and less as the minutes pass," Bellamy whispered, chuckling. He winced. "I hurt... *everywhere*."

"The docs said it would be a few weeks before you were close to normal again."

"Is there a close to normal ever again after this?"

"Probably not," Quinn whispered before pressing a kiss to Bellamy's forehead. "A new normal maybe."

Bellamy lifted his stare... just as the babe let out a wail.

"Sounds hungry to me," Joel said, bringing Carter to the bed.

Bellamy adjusted himself a little and pulled open the hospital gown before taking their son into his arms. "Here goes nothing."

He brought Carter to his chest... and the babe instinctively latched on and began to nurse.

Joel caressed the babe's head. "They know what to do most of the time."

"Am I doing it right?"

Joel nodded. "Yep."

Quinn watched his son nursing, and his chest tightened up. Tears stung the backs of his eyes... and he knew his heart was ready to burst. He held his little family close... promising the gods above he would provide and protect.

Just as he'd vowed on their mating day.

"So which one of you is next?" Tolliver asked.

Quinn looked up, seeing his grandfather looking toward the blank stares on Beau and Tanner's faces.

"Not it!" Tanner cried before jumping up, eyeing Fitz, and leaving the room.

Quinn frowned as he watched Fitz quickly follow his brother out, an odd look to the alpha's face.

"You don't think…?" Bellamy murmured before looking at Quinn. "Nah… *couldn't* be."

THE END

Kelex

Coming 31 May 2019

Unexpected Heat
An Omegaverse Short
Omega Quadrant, 1.5

You asked for more Gray and Rohan… well here they are…

Gray and Rohan Parker have been through one hell of a year. After a mating that started out with both life and death, they've held on tight to one another for months, just trying to find a way through. Needing some alone time, Rohan plans a lavish vacation for two in paradise—the honeymoon they weren't able to take. Now that their twins are fifteen-months-old, they hope to finally connect again and share an intimacy they haven't been able to since the toddlers came to be.

But a mix-up with the luggage threatens their little piece of paradise and brings up old fears and buried emotions. They face issues of loss, love, and their future together—and have to decide if they let nature take its course during an unexpected heat.

Coming later in 2019

His Reluctant Omega
An Omegaverse Book
Omega Quadrant, 2

Omega Avery Stephens refuses to be the compliant, submissive mate he was raised to be. He's tired of being told he's less than and will have to wait for an alpha to come and 'save' him.

After his fathers die in a tragic accident, he must stand up and be responsible for his younger omega brothers. Knowing their savings will only go so far, he looks to the future. Avery will need an income and not the pittance an omega makes. He shears his long locks, purchases illegal scent blockers, and lies his way into college under the pseudonym Abraham Norcross, a beta.

Avery does everything in his power to prove an omega can be more than 'a womb with legs' but when he comes across his alpha, he struggles not to be the stereotypical weak and needy omega. Yet all he wants to do is go to his knees and beg the man to fill him with a child.

Can he find a path somewhere between heaven and hell—and still hold on to his self-respect?

Kelex

ABOUT THE AUTHOR

International bestselling gay erotica/erotic romance author Kelex lives in Hampton Roads with her twenty-something slacker kidult and two semi-loveable masses of fur who are often found snarling at the mailman or UPS driver—or pooping on the brand new carpet.

When not being a pain in her daughter's ass, a gardening goddess, the baker of bread, the master of cake disaster, or the drinker of *allllll* the coffee, she writes under various pen names all over the erotica and erotic romance genre map.

NEW FROM KELEX

Want to stay up to date with new releases?
Join Kelex's monthly newsletter!

http://eepurl.com/dvS2_X

One Wild Heat

Twisted E-Publishing, LLC
www.twistedepublishing.com

Printed in Dunstable, United Kingdom

64179121R00133